A Spirit Flame Novel

I0586974

AZURE BLAZE

ELIZABETH C. NATALIA

D.o.l.l.
M N I S L L S

Daughters of Love & Light
www.dollministries.com
Adelaide, South Australia
info@dollministries.com

© Elizabeth C. Natalia 2023

ISBN: 978-0-6455086-3-5 (paperback)

Publisher's Note: This novel is a work of fiction. Names, characters, places, and incidents are either products of the author's imagination or used fictitiously. All characters are fictional, and any similarity to people living or dead is purely coincidental.

Cataloguing-in-Publications entry is available from the National Library of Australia http:/catalogue.nla.gov.au

First Edition published 2023

for Jenny Glazebrook and Wendy Parker
the prayer warriors who help me raise my sword.

Set me as a seal upon your heart,
as a seal upon your arm;
for love is as strong as death,
jealousy is fierce as the grave,
its flashes are flashes of fire,
the very flame of the LORD.

CONTENTS

CHAPTER 1

Spiritual GPS

Her eyes stung. Blinking away tears, Crystina rode into the night. Questions spun in her mind, the loudest a mere three letter word. *Why?* After everything the enemy had taken from her, why did *he* have to go too?

She gripped the handles until her armored gloves began to pinch. "You are still good," she whispered from between gritted teeth. "You are still good."

Crystina still wore the old Kevlar gear Papi bought her from the vintage shop; the sort that made her look like a rev-head. Vivid blue flames curled down the arms of the jacket, spreading like wings across its back. When she had protested, saying she could just drive, he told her, "No granddaughter of mine is going to clunk around on four wheels."

That was the day Abuela gave Crystina her crucifix. "Here, wear this if you're going to go out on that machine of his..."

Crystina hadn't understood Papi's love of motorbikes at the time.

But she did now.

Crystina knew that in moments such as these, there were two choices. Run from God. Or run to God. And she wanted to *ride* to Him.

Churning the throttle to life, she eased onto Juniper Bay's esplanade. Night sea winds barreled from her left. Turning onto main street toward old Juniper town, she coasted over cracked pavement and past abandoned buildings and warehouses. A faint breeze tousled the hair hanging loose from beneath her helmet. And here, a strange vision appeared in her mind's eye— a road beneath the old bridge. She had only been there once before, when she took the subway to school, got off at the wrong stop, and ended up in no-man's land.

Go. Now.

It wasn't audible but she knew it was *Him.*

"Jesus? What is this, some sort of spiritual navigation?"

He didn't respond.

So, she did what any girl would do when the Holy Spirit captured her thoughts. She rode to that half-dead place in the middle of the night on a whisper that God might meet her there.

Fighting fear and every logical thought, she rode through backstreets to reach the shadowy road beneath the bridge. Squinting, she searched for a sign. Something to tell her she was listening to God's Spirit and not going crazy. Security cameras winked like stray stars overhead—no doubt they were broken by now. No one used this road. Well, almost no one. The motorbike rumbled to a slow roll, and Crystina lowered her feet to steady it, treading the pavement. She switched off the headlight, wishing her eyes would adjust to the blackness and see whatever God had brought her here to see. Unless He hadn't. Maybe it was just the harsh reality of the last two days weighing on her? She had heard grief could make people do strange things, but this had to be a new extreme. Riding to some forsaken place in the middle of the night, not having the sense to tell anyone where she went, and—

A woman's scream rang out, echoing through the piers. Shadows shifted in the distance. Struggling. She revved the motorbike to life and kicked off the ground as it lurched ahead. *Jesus, help me.*

As she closed in on them, she caught a glimpse of aqua scrubs—the uniform of old Juniper town hospital. A broad dark figure overshadowed the nurse.

Without a second thought, she shouted, "Hey!"

The voice that left her lips was far more commanding than the teenage girl it belonged to. There was a growl in it. A strength she had never heard before.

3

And somehow, it struck fear in the attacker. He staggered back and, with a precision completely foreign to her, Crystina drifted toward the nurse, coming to a stop a fraction from her trembling body and creating a wall between her and the man in the ski mask.

Crystina held out her hand and pulled the nurse onto the rear of the motorbike. Then together they sped into the night and the man bolted in the opposite direction.

Crystina's heart thumped in her chest. It was all she could hear. Far louder than the roar of the engine.

She waited until they arrived in the heart of Juniper City ignited by streetlamps before pulling up to the curb outside the police station.

Still shaken, the nurse slowly staggered to the pavement.

"Are you okay?" Crystina asked.

She stared, clutching her bag to her body. "He must've been waiting for me. When I finished my shift... That has never happened..."

"But are you okay?"

With a shake of her head, she finally nodded. "Yes, yes... thanks to you."

"Head inside and tell the cops what happened. I gotta go."

"Wait—"

But how could she? How could she explain what happened? God *told* her to go there? Besides, she had just travelled with a helmet-less passenger.

As Crystina made her way back to the lighthouse, her spirit was aflame. A deep burning. It hadn't been there before. In fact, the only other time she'd felt it was in the waters of baptism in Juniper Bay two years before. It wasn't just internal anymore though. Now, it was revealing itself in goosebumps down her arms—she didn't have to remove her jacket to know. And there was a lightness to her body—and to her spirit—that had only known heaviness for what seemed like forever.

Crystina didn't remember a time before grief, before she lost her parents and brothers in a single night. She didn't know if this lightness existed in her earliest childhood and the Lord was now using this new season of grief to connect her to the girl she used to be. But something was shifting inside her. And after her raw heart had experienced the Holy Spirit in such a miraculous and tangible way, Crystina knew He was bringing her to a point of no return.

There was one person she wanted to tell. One person she couldn't help but tell. So she took one more detour on her joy ride with God.

Once in Juniper Bay, Crystina pulled into the side-street off the esplanade to an old family home she knew almost as well as her own. Leaving the motorbike and helmet a short way off, she waded through the bushes and long grass. He would be awake. He had to be. She knew all too well he studied around the clock these days. Which was why she'd hardly seen him lately.

She slipped off her gloves and knocked on the bedroom window like she used to when they'd sneak out to swim in the bay, back when they had no shame. She still remembered the night they were caught and told that soon things would change, and it wouldn't be appropriate for them to behave like children anymore. There had been less talk about their sneaking out and more about their lack of clothing. Crystina hadn't understood back then.

But she did now.

Jeremiah came to the window, his bare arms flexing as he shoved it open above his head. She hadn't seen him without a shirt since last summer and she couldn't remember him looking like *that*. He leaned across the windowsill and pulled her into a hug.

"I'm so sorry, Crys," he whispered into her hair.

Then it hit her like an oncoming train. That scent. Soap, fresh laundry, and a hint of Old Spice. She breathed deeply, grateful he couldn't see her on the border of madness. And with her exhale, her confident facade was obliterated, leaving her raw and vulnerable. Her hands rested on his warm dark skin and a new wave of guilt crashed over her. Papi was gone. And for the briefest moment, she had forgotten.

"Are you okay?" he asked, pulling away to study her face.

She swallowed hard. How could she tell him now?

"I'm sorry." She shook her head. "I just wanted to see you."

"Of course, here."

Crystina took his arm, and he helped her climb in through the window into the dark room. Even in the middle of the night, she could tell everything was in its place. It was a good thing JCU didn't insist on students residing on campus, Jeremiah wouldn't have coped with a roommate. He barely restrained himself from commenting when Crystina's odd socks were visible. Yes, everything was in its place. Except Jeremiah. He had just been rudely taken from his.

"You were asleep. I should go..."

"Crys." He reached to switch on his lamp. "It's fine. Sit down. Are you okay?"

She shrugged out of her jacket and joined him on the bed, trying to meet his eye without her gaze falling to his bare chest. What was wrong with her? This was Jerry. Her best friend. "How's study going?"

"Exhausting," he breathed. "Sorry I haven't been around much."

She had missed him. She missed his presence and the smell of him. But she couldn't tell *him* that. "It's okay."

"Then when Abuela called today, I wasn't sure if you would want to see me or if you just wanted to be alone..."

She opened her mouth to speak, but he continued.

"I just—" He stopped himself, his hand falling to his side. "I wasn't sure what you needed. And I should know. I should—"

"Jerry," she blurted, "I didn't come here because of what happened to Papi."

He adjusted himself on the bed, his forehead creased. "Then, why did you come?"

"I feel bad even mentioning it on a day like today but..."

"Hey, you can tell me anything. You know that, right?"

She nodded. "Yeah, well, it may sound crazy but..."

He eased himself a little closer.

"I went on a ride with the Holy Spirit tonight."

He arched a brow. "Excuse me?"

"I know, it sounds nuts, right? But I totally saved this nurse, and there was this man attacking her and..." Crystina stared into his immense dark eyes, uncertain of what she was seeing. Did he believe her? She sighed. "Should I just go now?"

He relaxed a little, settling into his pillow. "I thought—" He shook his head. "Start at the beginning."

"Okay, but then I promise, I'm going to let you sleep."

Crystina was grateful for the space he held for her. No judgement because she wasn't crying. She was still grieving, he knew that. But he let her feel the joy of what she'd just experienced to the full and it just made her want to stay by his side for as long as possible.

But tomorrow held different plans for the two of them, and they both needed their sleep. So once she described every detail of her ride with God, Crystina hugged him and pulled her jacket back on. If only to cover the goosebumps that had returned like an unbroken fever.

CHAPTER 2

Accidents Happen

Two Days Earlier

"You'll be late for work!" Abuela called from the kitchen.

Crystina glanced at the clock and snapped her journal shut. The thick tattered Bible wilted closed, then landed on her bed with an almighty thud. Crystina had woken before the sun. How was it already 8am?

She tugged on her heavy boots then thumped down the spiral staircase and through the living area to the front door.

Abuela tutted. "You know, breakfast is the most important meal of the day."

Crystina pulled on her motorcycle jacket. "I don't have time."

"Always in such a rush." Papi leisurely turned a wide page in his newspaper and eased back into the dining chair, his breakfast plate empty. "I'm exhausted just watching you."

"Some of us have to work."

He shrugged. "Some of us have to go fishing."

"And some of us need to make sure we all eat!" Abuela waved her wooden spoon. "Crystina, if you're going to die on that machine, I'd rather it be on a full stomach."

"Ah, leave her alone." Papi waved his hand out from behind the newspaper.

"What happened to taking the subway, eh?" Abuela asked. "I thought we agreed you would take the subway."

"We did—and I *do*—but I'm running late." Crystina weaved past the couch to kiss Papi's cheek before retrieving her helmet. "I gotta go. Love you both."

"And we love you," Papi said. "But, Crystina?"

She paused at the door.

He peered over the black and white print and lowered his glasses. "Be careful, hmm?"

She grinned. "Always."

Crystina tried to keep her promise as she left the lighthouse. When she thundered past the Sanderson home, she tried not to let her frustration impact the

11

throttle. But as soon as she saw the home she once knew as well as her own, she tensed and her heart ached. She hadn't seen Jeremiah in months. He'd been in his own world. They were supposed to be best friends and yet there she had been, a few steps across the bay, just waiting for him to have time for her again. She wondered if he had a girlfriend and maybe she was keeping him occupied. Crystina wasn't interested in a relationship. She didn't see the point. It was just a recipe for heartache. She would only set herself up to lose someone again.

When she reached old Juniper town, a strange gut-instinct told her to take the backstreets and head past the old stone church where her family was buried.

She shook her head. *This is not the morning.*

But the sensation flared up again and she could almost see the exact place in her mind's eye. *What sort of prompting is that, Holy Spirit? You're going to make me late...*

Ignoring the strange feeling, she veered onto the highway and headed straight for Juniper City.

Once in the carpark adjoining the office building of Legion International Media, she removed her gear, stored it in her locker, and found a scrunchie and a crumpled suit jacket. Anything to hide her helmet hair and sweat patches.

"What's going on?" She entered the tearoom at five minutes to nine, her hot-mess hair now tamed, her jacket still warm from the hand drier in the ladies' bathroom.

"Another woman was attacked in broad daylight." Emma stared wide-eyed at the small television set.

Crystina paused at the push-button coffee machine, her finger hovering. "*Really?*"

"Yeah, apparently near St Peter's church in old Juniper town." She gulped a mouthful of coffee.

Crystina leaned against the cupboard. "That's not far from me."

Emma cradled her cup in both hands. "It's a bit scary. I hope they catch whoever did it."

"Are you going to use that?" Amos Xavier asked, appearing by the coffee machine.

Crystina practically jumped away from him. "Oh, no, I mean, here, let me make you a coffee. You shouldn't have to make your own..."

"I'll manage," he said. He took the cup from her hand and retrieved another from the shelf. His fingers brushed hers for a moment. Then he placed both cups under the dispenser and pushed the button twice.

Mr. Xavier handed her the cup of coffee and watched the television screen. He took a single sip of his own, winced in disgust, then poured the contents down the sink. He cocked his head for a moment then said. "When you're settled, can I please see you in my office?"

She gulped. "Of course."

Emma watched him leave the tearoom. "Wow. That's weird. He never wants to see anyone!"

"Well, wish me luck." Crystina held out her fist.

Emma bumped it with her own before fanning her fingers. "You've got this."

Crystina waited seven minutes. Five felt too eager. Ten too negligent. Then she went to Amos Xavier's corner office. It was all glass and steel, so the entire floor could see her being summoned.

She cleared her throat and lingered awkwardly by his door. "Thanks for the coffee."

"Good, you're here." He forced a brief tight smile. "Come in. Sit down."

She perched on the edge of the sleek chair opposite him. His wide streamlined desk clearly defined the space between them. His plaque stated *Amos Xavier, Editor-in-Chief.*

He shuffled papers the way all handsome young businessmen do—pensively, intelligently, studying the paperwork just long enough to give an impressionable girl like her permission to snoop around uninterrupted. Unfortunately, there was nothing much to look at. He had no personal belongings to give any aspect of him away. No photographs. No pieces of art. Only stationery, files, and a bookcase of black spined books which appeared to be immaculately dusted if not read.

"So," he began. "I'm in the market for a personal assistant."

"Oh?" What was there possibly left to organize?

"Yes, I really don't know how much longer I can do without one. That coffee is just..." He cringed. "Let's just say, I need someone who can run small errands for me, that sort of thing."

Crystina nodded and tried to follow his train of thought. She thought a push-button machine at least produced better coffee than the tin canister of instant she used at home.

"So, I was thinking," he went on, "you could outsource and advertise on my behalf."

"Yeah," she said. "Of course."

"Great." He returned to the papers on his desk. "That'll be all."

"Oh, right." She made her way toward the door then paused. "Do you have any preferences?"

"Hmm." His mouth twitched. "Blonde?"

Her expression fell. "I mean, professional preferences, sir."

"Good memory?" He shrugged but didn't meet her eye. "To remember my coffee order, dry cleaning, that sort of thing."

She waited for more but evidently there was nothing else. So she headed back to her desk in hopes that this small task might fill her day. Sharing the role of a junior assistant with countless others had its perks but one of the downfalls was boredom. Since the government compensated these menial positions, the managers didn't seem to mind what the junior assistants did so long as it was somehow work related. That included reading competitive news sites for "research". Crystina had already scrolled aimlessly for two hours yesterday. At least Harper wasn't here today to make the boredom even more uncomfortable. Crystina didn't know why she had taken a personal day, but she was grateful.

Crystina had almost finished the job advertisement, trying to make it sound as professional as possible, when her phone vibrated.

She thought about not answering but when she glanced at the screen, the home phone number stared back at her.

"Hey, I'm working," she whispered, sinking in her seat between the dividers. She may have been bored but at Legion International Media, even boredom wasn't a good enough reason to take personal calls.

A sob echoed down the line.

"Abuela?" She jolted upright. "What's wrong?"

Emma's head peered up and over the divider. Concern strained her usually cheerful face.

Abuela released a shaky breath then said, "There has been an accident..."

CHAPTER 3

Q & A

"What are you doing here?"

The question hit Crystina with unusual force. Barely three days ago, she would have known the answer. But today she wasn't so sure. After all, two days had slipped by in a blur. Two days in a parallel universe of funeral arrangements and notices and reporting the news to distant family members who only seemed to appear for births, deaths, or marriages. Though, it seemed the only family news that ever came from Juniper Bay was that of death. Then, there had been last night. If Papi's death wasn't enough to question her lingering presence on this earth, then last night certainly did. What *was* she still doing here? And was last night's Spirit-led adventure part of the answer?

It was the second evocative question she had been asked that morning. The first had come from Abuela.

"Would you like to take communion with me?"

Crystina had paused at their weather-beaten front door.

Abuela cleared away the breakfast dishes then eased a plate with freshly baked flat bread onto the table followed by a decanter of grape juice.

"What's all this?"

"It is only you and I now." Her voice was heavy. "So, I am claiming the blood of Jesus Christ over our household. For protection."

Crystina swiftly went to kiss her soft leathery cheek. "Papi's death was not your fault."

"He is not the reason," she said softly, pointing to the box television set on mute.

Crystina followed the imaginary line from Abuela's index finger to the screen. A headline beamed back at her. *The blue flame rider! Hero or accomplice?*

"She saved me," read the captions beneath the face of the familiar nurse. "She's a hero without a doubt."

She fell into the chair beside Abuela as she watched the glitchy security camera footage, reduced to slow motion for dramatic affect.

The blue flame?

"I can explain," she whispered and hoped it was true.

18

"I woke up this morning," Abuela began gently, "and the Lord spoke in my spirit and gave me a strange peace. I wasn't sure why He had given it to me, until I saw the news... Then I knew what I had to do. I had to claim the blood of Christ over you." She nodded as she opened her heavy worn-out Bible. "You must understand, Crystina, that it is at moments such as these—when one's heart is exposed—that God can work the most incredible miracles."

"I'll take communion with you." Crystina gazed down at the black and blood-red lettered page, opened to the book of first Corinthians.

"... and when He had given thanks, He broke it and said,
'This is my body, which is for you; do this in remembrance of
me.'
In the same way, after supper he took the cup, saying,
'This cup is the new covenant in my blood:
do this, whenever you drink it, in remembrance of me.'
For whenever you eat this bread and drink this cup,
you proclaim the Lord's death until He comes."
I CORINTHIANS 11:24-26

"So, what are you doing here?" Harper repeated, dragging Crystina back to the present moment at Legion International Media. "Your grandfather just died. I'm sure you could have taken a personal day."

Who told her? On second thought, it didn't matter.

"I just needed some normalcy." Crystina attempted a smile and kept her head down toward her desk.

"Whatever," Harper scoffed. "Always the hero..."

The crease in Crystina's brow deepened. If Abuela was here, she'd tell her to stop before the wind changed and her face stayed that way. Abuela might have been a great prayer warrior, but those old time superstitions died hard.

"Good morning!" Emma popped her head up over the divider.

Crystina flinched.

"Sorry." She made a sweet cringing face. "But don't mind her. I think Harper's just the mean girl type, to be honest."

She hadn't always been that way.

"Yeah, did I ever tell you we actually went to school together?" Crystina asked.

"No, but lucky you." Emma giggled then whipped out her phone. "But speaking of heroes, did you hear about the blue flame rider?"

Before Crystina could reply, Emma thrust her phone in front of her so Crystina was staring at a blurry online video of herself effortlessly pulling the nurse onto the back of her motorbike.

Emma watched over her shoulder. "I wonder who she is..."

"Flower delivery for Crystina Santos!" a voice called.

She stood instantly, hand in the air like a first grader, grateful for the interruption. "Here."

"I didn't know you had a *boyfriend*?" Emma watched Crystina open the card, her giggle broken up with a small snort.

For the first time that morning, Crystina smiled. For real. "I don't, it's just Jerry." She shrugged. "We've been friends for forever."

Just not in the three months she'd worked with Emma Dunkirk. But Crystina needed to say it out loud—friends, *just* friends—so neither she nor Emma got the wrong idea. It didn't matter how good he had looked last night. He was her best friend. Nothing was going to change that. Crystina didn't want to lose anyone else. Especially him.

For the briefest moment, she caught Harper staring. To be more specific, Jerry had been *their* best friend until senior year had turned Harper into someone they no longer recognized, and she upgraded to richer friends. On scholarship, Jerry and Crystina were always out of place. But Harper didn't have to be. Somehow, Crystina and Harper had ended up as junior assistants for the same media firm while Jeremiah Sanderson was living the dream at JCU. But he wasn't too big of a university hot shot just yet to completely forget about

Crystina—even if he would have been sleep deprived from her visit last night.

The note was beautifully understated.

Praying for you.
Always + Forever,
Jerry.

Just as Crystina reached for her phone to text him, Xavier strode into the open plan office, his piercing eyes searching the rows of desks.

"*You, you,* and *you,* my office. Now." He pointed directly at Harper, Emma, then Crystina before his stare landed on the flowers on her desk. "Unless you have something more important to do?"

She quickly stowed her phone away in her purse. "No, sir."

Without another word, he walked away.

Emma jerked her head and Crystina followed. Harper walked ahead of them into the glass-walled corner office, letting the door fall closed behind her. Emma awkwardly pushed her way in and held the door open.

"All my fact checkers apparently have their hands full." He grunted, rolling his eyes. "So I need the three of you to work together to find this *blue flame* character. Search social media. Talk to your friends. Whatever you young people do these days. I want him found."

Him? Surely, no one mistook her for a guy?

"They're actually saying she's a *she*." Emma giggled. "I mean, a woman... sir." She cleared her throat. "A young one, they're assuming, by her stature and posture..."

Amos Xavier stared her down for a long moment. "In journalism, we never assume anything."

"Yes, sir."

"But what if she doesn't want to be found?" Crystina asked.

He smirked. "We're going to turn her into a celebrity. Who wouldn't want that?" He took a step toward her.

"A lot of people wouldn't want that," she said before adding a respectful, "*sir.*"

"I'll find her," Harper said. "And I won't need *their* help to do it."

"I just want information. So, never discount valuable resources," he said. "You have until the end of the week, or you're all fired."

"What?" Crystina blurted.

He rounded his desk and sat down. "I suggest you all get to work."

She desperately tried to neutralize her facial expression. If she couldn't look pleasant, she at least didn't want to look furious. Crystina moved toward the door, though not before a scowl unceremoniously made its way onto her face.

"Santos, wait."

Harper paused at the door.

"Did I say Lloyd? No, not *you*." Amos Xavier grunted. "Santos."

Harper forced a tight smile, but Crystina recognized that slight heat in her cheeks, the sheen over her eyes.

"Good luck," Emma whispered as she made her escape.

He waited until they left. "Take a seat."

"I'm fine standing, thank you."

"Suit yourself." He leaned back in his chair. "How old are you?"

Her face twisted, giving away her thoughts before she even spoke. "Can't you look that up?"

"Santos. I asked how old you are."

She cleared her throat. "I'm eighteen, sir."

"Xavier," he corrected. "You're not attracted to me, are you?"

Crystina opened her mouth to speak but nothing came out.

He chuckled. "Okay, maybe you are then."

"No," she said quickly. "Not in the least. I was just surprised by your question."

"Oh, well, that's a little harsh, but good." His body visibly relaxed. "See, I have this problem with the junior assistants having crushes on me."

"You poor thing." Crystina couldn't tell him he was becoming less attractive by the moment.

"Yes, well, it has made it hard to promote any of them to my personal assistant. I don't suppose you're interested in the position?"

She couldn't help but think fetching his coffee and dry cleaning sounded more like a demotion. Besides, what had changed between Friday's instruction to outsource and today's sudden change of heart? A moment ago he was threatening to fire her.

"You haven't mentioned what happened to the last one," she said.

He stared up at her with those pale eyes most girls go crazy over. "She fell in love with me."

Fortunately, she wasn't most girls. "So, you fired her?"

"God, no. *Worse.* I dated her."

She cringed. "Well, if I'm going to work in any proximity to you, you will have to stop *that*."

"I know." He rolled his eyes. "I've learned my lesson—"

"No. You need to stop taking the Lord's name in vain."

"Oh." He stared at her again before realization dawned. "*Oh.* So, you're religious?"

"I'm a Christian. You can fire me now if you want."

"Santos, that would be discrimination."

"I know that." But she wouldn't put it past him.

"Find me something on this *blue blaze* character, and you have the position."

"It's blue flame," she muttered.

"Well, I like blaze better."

Her cheeks warmed and she changed the subject. "What about Emma? She's been here longer."

Now it was his turn to cringe. "She practically swoons around me."

"Well, what about my condition?"

"I'll smarten up my act. No more God's name in... whatever you said."

"In vain."

"Yes, *that.* Anything else?"

"I'm brunette."

"I won't hold that against you," he said.

And just like that, Crystina ran out of excuses. "Okay, well, besides my not being attracted to you, why *me?*"

"Because JCU was crazy not to accept you for their scholarship program after the grades you received last year."

She nodded slowly. "So, you have read my file."

"Aren't you angry at your god about that?"

"No. Because I know who did get accepted to the program, and if it was up to me, I would've chosen him too."

He studied her, swiveling slightly in his chair.

"Okay, I'm intrigued by you, Santos. Go get me some dirt on this superhero."

"*Superhero?*" She laughed it off. "I wouldn't say she's a *superhero...*"

"Well, that's how we're going to paint her alright. Front page." He spread his hands across the imaginary tabloid. "*Blue Blaze—Juniper City's own superhero.*" Then an idea seemed to flash across Xavier's eyes. "No... *Azure Blaze.*"

As much as Crystina didn't want to admit it, the name stirred something in her. Shivers exploded down her limbs. There was a flutter in her stomach, a slight lightness to her head.

She cleared her throat. "Azure Blaze?"

Even saying it out loud seemed to change something in her, as though she was making a promise.

"That's it." Xavier nodded in approval. "I need to get that to marketing asap. *Azure Blaze catching alight in Juniper City.*"

When Crystina returned to her desk, Emma was slumped in hers with her head in her hands.

"Hey, what's wrong?"

She lifted her head and smiled. "Nothing. I'm just always saying the wrong thing. Like, seriously Emma, *just stop*, am I right?" She forced a giggle, but it wasn't light and airy like before. Besides, her bloodshot eyes gave her away. "But it doesn't really matter, I'll probably be fired by the end of the week anyway."

Crystina squeezed in between the dividers and leaned against Emma's desk. She had no desire to give an interview, not even to save all three of their jobs. "Well, hypothetically speaking, if you *did* lose your job, what would you do? What did you dream of doing when you left school?"

"Journalism," she said, like there was no other answer.

Crystina gulped. She hadn't expected that.

"And I thought this was my big break," Emma went on, "my foot in the door without having to go to college. But, if I don't find anything on the blue flame, I'll be back to square one..."

"He's calling her *Azure Blaze* now."

"That's cool." Emma brightened for a moment. "But it still doesn't help me."

Crystina nodded slowly. Guilt niggled at her and she was acutely aware of the power that had been placed in her own inexperienced hands.

Part of her envied Emma for having such conviction. Crystina still had no idea what she wanted to do with her life. Although, last night had given her a taste of what a Spirit-led life could mean. Then again, it was a once off... right?

CHAPTER 4

The Sidekick

"You will seek me and find me
when you seek me with all your heart."
JEREMIAH 29:13

Jeremiah's knee bounced. His heel tapped, scatting to the beat of his thoughts as he sat at the solid family dining table. He had sat here countless times before, but this time it was different. This time someone was missing.

Abuela was still busying herself in the kitchen when Crystina arrived battling the dodgy front door. Now that Papi was gone, Jeremiah should fix it for them. In time. When they were ready for another man to step in and help. Of course, the newly appointed priest hadn't waited for such an invitation but had considered it his holy duty to visit the moment he heard the news of Papi's death. And Abuela, in typical fashion, had asked him to stay for dinner, before phoning Jeremiah to come and soften the evening for her beloved granddaughter.

Crystina.

When she finally burst into the lighthouse, Jeremiah's body seized. His fidgeting paused. Carrying the bouquet he had sent, she touched her hair with her free hand then brushed her high-waisted skirt. She hadn't expected company. There was a slight flush to her cheeks as though she'd been caught out of place. But she was perfect.

"Hi," she stammered, her gaze glued to the man in Papi's seat.

"You must be Crystina." He looked blankly in her general direction. "It's a pleasure to finally meet you. I hear you're a remarkable young lady."

She glanced at Jeremiah.

He shrugged.

"From your Abuela, of course." The priest smiled. "I have recently joined the parish of St Peter's in old Juniper town. I am the Watchman."

This visibly piqued her interest.

"I understand you are between congregations," the Watchman said.

Jeremiah and Crystina shared an uncertain look. Jeremiah's knee started to bounce again. He stole a glance at Crystina before she sat down beside him. He'd never seen her look so *professional*. Yes, that was it.

Wasn't it? His mouth tasted dry. He took a long drink of cold water.

"Abuela and I would like to check out Jerry's church next week," Crystina said. "Papi enjoyed a more traditional service, but we would like to try something... different."

Jeremiah flashed his lop-sided grin. "You make me sound like an alien."

"I just mean, I'll probably be the only white girl there," she said, playfully nudging him.

"Eh, you're more of a beigy color anyway."

She scowled at him, but it just widened his grin. Beige hadn't been the right color for her. Maybe caramel.

"Well, just know, you are always welcome at St Peters," the Watchman said. "All of you."

Without warning, Crystina shot up out of her chair and lunged toward the kitchen, just as Abuela dropped the oven dish. Ceramic smashed. Abuela's hands glowed as red as the tomato salsa splattered on the mosaic tiles. Crystina took Abuela by the arms and rushed her to the sink, while Abuela muttered in Spanish beneath her breath.

"Can I help?" the Watchman asked and reached for his walking aid.

"No, no." Abuela winced when her palms met the cool running water. "I wasn't concentrating."

Jeremiah quietly used the oven mitts to collect the hot shards of ceramic from the kitchen floor. He then cleared away dinner with a paper towel.

"I'm so sorry," the Watchman said. "I shouldn't have intruded tonight."

Abuela shook her head, seemingly preparing to belittle the interruption.

But Crystina said from over her shoulder, "Thank you for understanding."

And with that, the Watchman was subtly dismissed, guiding himself out the door with his aid and into the night. How he planned to serve the community with his vision so impaired, Jeremiah wasn't sure. But then again, he was more than a little distracted. Jeremiah found himself wishing he had Crystina's commanding presence. She didn't even know the power she possessed over people. He could only imagine the impact she made on the office. Grieving or not, she was always impressive. People were naturally drawn to her. Which was why Juniper City was turning her into a hero. Azure Blaze. It was everywhere. All over social media. The whole campus today had been talking about her, wondering who she was and what she was going to do next...

Jeremiah and Crystina excused themselves to the lantern room with a tray of Juniper Bay's best wood-oven pizza, made with love by his mom and delivered by

Jeremiah's youngest brother Isaac. Mom must've been listening to the Holy Spirit to send dinner over unannounced. She didn't cook gourmet like the Santos family, but she knew how to make a little go a long way between five kids on a single mom's wage, and pizza cooked to perfection outside in the sea air was her specialty.

"Abuela is exhausted," Crystina said.

"At least she's resting now." A string of melted cheese stretched from Jeremiah's mouth to the half-eaten slice of ham and pineapple.

Crystina cringed at him before digging into her half of pepperoni. "Fruit doesn't belong on pizza."

"We can agree to disagree." He swallowed hard. "So, did it happen again? In the kitchen just now?"

"Hmm? Oh, the whole Azure Blaze thing?" She nodded slowly. "The Holy Spirit told me to help but I didn't respond quick enough. It's my fault Abuela burnt her hands."

"I wouldn't say that. It's like saying it's your fault that man attacked the nurse, if you hadn't got there in time."

"But I did."

"And next time you will again."

She gazed out at the deepening sky beyond the pane. "It's almost time."

"Yeah. Are you ready?"

"I've helped Papi do it a thousand times."

"That's not what I asked, Crystina." He turned to face her, grateful for the pizza tray on the floor between them. It was the only thing keeping him from reaching for her. That and the fact that his action might stray into the unknown territory beyond best mate protocol. But there in the twilight and with her sad eyes, it was almost worth it.

"I'm ready." She forced a smile.

He leapt to his feet before holding his hands out to her. She pulled herself up, letting him take her full weight. He braced for it. The first time, in middle school, it might have taken him by surprise, but not now. Now he was used to her, even if he didn't see her as often as he would like. And she was used to him. A little too much, it seemed.

He watched as she set herself to work. Her hair hung loose now, released from the tight business ponytail she had sported when she first came home. Her shirt was untucked, and her heels were long stowed away in the closet downstairs. Her bare feet pattered, only restricted by the skirt that hugged her curves almost down to her knees. Jeremiah turned to face the ocean, hoping its cool spray might reach him up there.

"There," she announced and the scene before him ignited.

She curled up on the floor beneath the beacon, returning to her pepperoni pizza. "Aren't you going to finish your fruit salad?"

He grinned. *Jesus, help me. Help me not to fall in love with my best friend.*

Over pizza and a thermos of tea, Jeremiah and Crystina watched the beam of light rotate the way they used to with Papi. Quietly. Reverently. Brooding clouds shimmered for a moment before blackness took hold once more. Buoys floating on the waves blinked with a flash of orange until they were lost again a moment later. Then, as if from nowhere, the wind picked up, stirring the ocean. And in that moment, Crystina dropped her last slice of pizza.

"You okay?" he asked.

Her eyes glazed over.

He gave her a little shake. "Hey?"

She blinked. "I gotta go."

With unexpected speed, she descended the stairs by two, accidentally tearing her skirt. He followed, all the way down to the adjoining garage where she changed into her motorcycle gear, though not before shedding her office clothes. Jeremiah averted his now blissfully tainted gaze, fixing his attention on Papi's vintage jacket hanging by the roller door.

"I'm coming too."

She didn't respond but by the time she was on her bike, he was climbing up behind and securing the spare helmet. The roller door chugged open and Crystina— Azure Blaze—accelerated straight toward it. Jeremiah ducked to miss the metal panel's labored ascent.

Crystina's brunette waves smothered his helmet screen. His hands rested on her defined waist. Even in Kevlar she looked feminine. Womanly. He shook his head. God was calling her on a mission, and he was going to be there to witness it. *Concentrate, Jerry.* He silently scolded himself before praying again. *Jesus. Please. Help me not to fall in love with my best friend.*

Crystina maneuvered the motorbike as though Jeremiah were invisible. Feather-light. His presence didn't affect her turns or her determination for a moment. He leaned with her, confident in her hands. He trusted her. But more importantly, he trusted the One she followed.

In the early evening bustle of Juniper City, Crystina pulled to the curb and killed the engine. Jeremiah knew this place. He knew this street. He had ordered flowers to be sent here that morning.

"What are we doing here?" he asked, his voice muffled through the helmet.

"I don't know, this is just what I saw. Wait a minute, is that—"

"What?"

"The businessman. Twelve o'clock. That's Xavier."

"Maybe he forgot something?"

"Yeah, maybe..."

As though sensing he was being watched, Xavier paused and looked around. His stare firmly landed on them. Crystina gasped. But the tension was short lived.

Soon their presence had drawn more than just his attention and teenagers on the street came running over, cars pulled up a few meters ahead, smart phones appeared followed swiftly by flashes of white light. Xavier disappeared into the crowd, and Crystina ignited the engine and pulled back into the traffic. She rode hard. Jeremiah's hands clasped her waist as she weaved through backstreets back to old Juniper town. There she pulled up in a forgotten alley.

When she removed her helmet, her cheeks were flushed. "Well, that was weird."

"Yeah, I thought that Xavier guy would be at the front of the line wanting to take your photo."

"Azure Blaze's photo," she corrected.

"Yeah."

Although by her expression, he wondered if there was more to it. Was that the kind of guy she was attracted to? He didn't know. She'd never introduced him to a boyfriend and always kept anyone interested at arm's length. The fact that she tolerated Jeremiah was only due to their childhood friendship that had grown with them. "What's wrong?"

"Maybe I heard wrong? Maybe I wasn't listening properly?" She shook her head. "But I was sure—" She began to pace. "And why didn't he take my photo? Or try to corner me? That's what the Xavier I met today would have done."

"Is that what you wanted?"

"No." She scoffed. "You know I hate stuff like that."

"Yeah, I know, but maybe for him..."

"You can't be serious."

"He looks like a pretty well-to-do kind of guy."

"If that's what you think I'm looking for, you don't know me at all." The words had to have rolled off her tongue uncensored because a moment later, she pressed her fingers to her mouth. "I'm sorry. I don't know why I said that. I'm just frustrated."

"With me?"

"No... with God." She breathed. "Why would He take me there for no reason? And if there is a reason, why wouldn't He be clearer, like—"

"Sssh." Jeremiah held up his hand, listening. Perhaps it was just the wind? No, there it was again. A faint cry. Without a second thought, he was at Crystina's side, his arm protectively curled around her.

She pressed herself closer and whispered, "What is it?"

"You can't hear that?" he replied, equally as quiet.

There was a rustle by the abandoned garbage cans.

"Who's there?" Jeremiah demanded.

Another rustle.

A whimper.

Crystina relaxed beside him and stepped forward. She crouched and stretched out her arm expectantly, her palm facing the pavement. "It's okay," she said softly. A four-legged figure crawled out from the dark, all paws and limbs, matted fur, and bone.

Jeremiah lowered to whisper to her. "It could have rabies."

"It doesn't," she said, her eyes glistening in the moonlight. She beamed up at him. "*He* is why God called us out tonight."

Jeremiah's lopsided grin returned. "For a puppy?"

"Well, He feeds the sparrow, right?" She turned to the mixed-breed canine, her hand still outstretched. "It's okay."

The puppy staggered toward her and sniffed the tips of her fingers.

"Hey there..." Crystina breathed then she looked up pleadingly at Jeremiah. "Can you take him home? The lighthouse isn't really the place for a dog."

He wanted to say yes. Just to make her happy. But he knew better than to make empty promises. "I don't think Mom could handle another mouth to feed right now."

"Oh of course, forget I said anything."

Jeremiah wished he could provide for his family. For Crystina. Heck, even for this malnourished dog. He knew one day, when he finished his degree, he could get a higher-paying job. Things would be different. His mom wouldn't have to struggle anymore. And Crystina wouldn't have to stay at the lighthouse plagued by memories of her family and the accident. He might never be as successful as the man he'd seen on the street—*Xavier*—but God would help him provide for those he loved. Why else would Jeremiah have received the scholarship? It was God's provision. It had to be.

He looked over at Crystina, her sad eyes had returned. He would do anything to dispel them. Even try to talk his mom into having a dog.

"Crys, what's wrong?" he asked

"It's silly but..." A faint smile curled her lips as the puppy licked her hand. "I'm scared to take him to the lighthouse. What if something happens to him there?"

He knew what she was saying. What if he drowned? Like her parents. Like her brothers. Like Papi when he'd had his heart attack fishing in the water. The autopsy had shown the heart attack had been mild, but it was enough to throw him off balance, to leave him vulnerable to his surroundings. It was no wonder Crystina hated the water and didn't want to subject another creature to it.

"Dogs are great swimmers," Jeremiah said brightly.

She wiped her cheeks with the back of her hand, and it just about crushed him. He hadn't noticed she'd been crying.

"Really?" she asked.

"Yeah, haven't you heard of the doggy paddle? It comes naturally to them. God's design. Dogs are practically made for the water."

The clouds in her eyes lifted. "Well, in that case."

"Only..." Jeremiah glanced at the motorbike. "How are we going to get him there?"

She shrugged. "Walk." And with a brush of Jeremiah's arm, she bent down and lifted the pup into her arms. He watched her carry him to the motorbike. She then tossed a grin over her shoulder. "You'll have to push Papi's old beast though."

As she stood there caressing the puppy, moonlight streamed over her, and Jeremiah did what any man in his right mind would do. He reached for his phone and snapped a photo. The blue flames on her jacket seemed even brighter on the screen. Her hair was full and tousled—so much for helmet hair. Then he noticed something strange. He pinched and squeezed the photo, trying to see the number plate of Papi's motorbike. Very strange. He took several more photos, this time zooming in on the motorbike. But in every photo the same thing happened.

"Hey, check this out..."

She came over and glanced down at his phone. "You're taking photos of me?"

"Look at the bike. Notice anything?"

"The number plate." She breathed. "It's blurry in every photo."

"No matter how many I take. There's no way of reading it."

Crystina's mouth gaped before twitching into a smile. *"What?!* That's crazy."

Shivers spread down his arms, and he beamed at her. "I know. Crazy."

She shook her head, turned and, with a bounce in her step, made her way back up the alley. Jeremiah pushed the motorbike into a roll. He was going to have to pull an all-nighter to catch up on study, but it was worth it.

CHAPTER 5

Double Life

The day began on her knees. Silent prayers rose from Crystina's heart, and she watched God turn the sky from indigo to red. She held her mother's Bible with both hands, squeezing it as though new life would seep out of it and into her. Melchizedek snored from her bed, his tummy full of milk and mince. She'd have to buy him proper dog food. He and Crystina had a lot in common. They were both orphans. They both needed sustenance. His had come in the form of full-fat milk and Abuela's leftovers, hers from basking in God's presence. The Lord's mercies were new every morning and she desperately needed them today.

Abuela didn't ask any questions when she saw Chizzy lapping milk from a soup bowl. She quietly cleared the breakfast dishes, careful of her skirt and suit jacket. She almost had a mother-of-the-bride look to her, were the ensemble not black. Crystina watched Abuela reset the table for communion, complete with freshly baked flat bread. Crystina smoothed a thin dark jumper on over her work shirt before setting herself down beside Abuela—the last thing she needed was grape juice on her only clean shirt.

The morning slipped by in a haze, a dark haze, and by the time Crystina arrived at the office, it was well past lunch.

"What time do you call this?" Xavier snapped.

He appeared out of nowhere, catching her off guard. Her head felt heavy. She hadn't even cried when Jeremiah had read Papi's eulogy. What sort of granddaughter didn't cry at her grandfather's funeral? The Watchman had taken the service, focusing on the wonders of God's heavenly realms and what Papi's perfected eyes must be seeing now. Abuela wore black sunglasses and kept the tears for her beloved sacred.

"*Well*, Santos?"

"She completed a form with HR." Emma popped her head up over the divider in her typical meerkat routine. "It was approved yesterday."

"I didn't ask you."

"But she—"

Xavier glared at her. "She can speak."

"Crystina," Jeremiah's voice settled over the office. "Here, you left this at the church."

She looked up and gratitude swelled within her. Xavier stepped back as Jeremiah rested her purse on the desk.

"I thought you might need it," Jeremiah said to her, but his stare was fixed on Xavier.

"Thank you," Crystina said softly.

Harper stood. "Hey Jerry."

He glanced at her then back to Xavier before settling on Crystina. "Is everything okay?"

Xavier scoffed. "I didn't know you needed a bodyguard at work, Santos."

"Her name is *Crystina*," Jeremiah said. "And you might want to cut her some slack considering she came into the office after her grandfather's funeral."

Xavier's face twitched for a moment then he rolled his eyes and strode back to his office.

"You didn't have to do that," Crystina said.

"I know."

"You probably *shouldn't* have done that."

"I know," he breathed. "Want me to try to fix it?"

Crystina could just imagine how that would go down. "I'll do it. See you later?"

"Sure."

It took everything in her to get her out of that chair and follow Xavier to his office. And even more to

45

leave her pride and her grief at the threshold. "Sorry I was late."

Xavier grunted.

"Do you have anything on Azure Blaze?" she asked, changing the subject. "I heard she was near the office last night."

"I'm not going to do your job for you, Santos," he said, not looking away from the paper-thin computer monitor. "If there's a point to this conversation, I suggest you make it quickly."

"So, you didn't see her here last night?"

"I do have a life, you know." He glanced at her. "As hard as that may be to believe."

Crystina nodded. She didn't understand his need for secrecy but sensed she needed to let it rest. For now.

"I have a life too," she said. "And if I'm going to be your assistant, you're going to need to understand that."

"I haven't offered you the position yet."

"But you will," she said. "Because after today, I can safely say I will never find you attractive in any way, shape or form."

This got his attention. His brows rose. "Bravo, Santos. So, you do have a backbone."

"You have no idea." She turned to leave but spun around at the last minute. "And another thing, you may want to be nicer to Emma. Apparently, she may have some information on Azure Blaze..."

"I need facts, Santos," he snapped. "Not hear-say."

Could she really be this man's assistant? He infuriated her. He brought out the worst in her. Crystina wanted to tell him exactly what he could do with the position but then remembered a sobering thought—her battle was not against flesh and blood. Her battle was not against Amos Xavier. A spiritual battle was raging around her and in this state of heightened reliance on God, she knew the enemy would want to derail her. Distract her. Discourage her. Devastate her.

That was when she felt the tears begin to rise. So instead of mustering a sassy response, Crystina left without another word. She marched to the elevator, her finger smashing on the button to close the doors. When she arrived at the lobby, tears brimming, she found the building's reception desk empty. So, she took the phone and dialed the extension one numeral different from her own.

"This is Emma," she chirped. "How can I be of assistance?"

"It's Azure Blaze."

"What?!" Emma's squeal echoed down the line.

"Wanna meet?"

Crystina leaned against Papi's motorbike and watched through the helmet screen as Emma practically skipped toward her. Meeting beneath the bridge in old Juniper town had been Crystina's idea, if only to inspire Emma's article. If there was anyone at Legion International Media who she trusted to do her story justice, it was her.

"Hi Emma."

"Um, hi... *Azure Blaze.*" Emma beamed. She whipped out her phone, tapped a button, then placed it gently on the pavement. "I hope this is okay? I don't want to misquote you."

"Of course."

Emma exhaled shakily. "I'm sure I'm going to regret saying this but... I'm not actually a journalist yet. And there are probably one thousand better writers out there you could be speaking to."

She smiled behind the helmet. "I'm sure there are, but a friend of mine tells me you're a fan, so..."

"Well, I do have every newspaper clipping in my scrapbook at home," Emma confessed. "Like, not in a creepy way, it's just..." She paused, took a breath to steady herself, then said with shiny eyes, "You're an inspiration. Who knows what would have happened to that woman had you not been there. How did you even know she was there?"

She took a sharp breath. "God told me."

Emma's eyebrows shot up. "*God?*"

"Yeah, do you know Him?"

"Um, yeah, you could say that." Emma let out a nervous laugh.

It was a conversation they hadn't had until now and Emma would have thought she was telling a complete stranger. Perhaps that's what made it safe.

"I guess I just wasn't expecting that *you* knew Him," Emma went on. "Wow! We're like, totally sisters in Christ!"

Crystina couldn't control her grin. "We are. Totally." She nodded. "Well, see, that night God literally put this place in my mind, and He has led me in other ways since."

"Wait, you mean, by the Holy Spirit?"

"Yeah."

"So, the Spirit of God tells you what to do?"

"He also kind of does it through me," Crystina explained. "I have no idea how I pulled off that drift, I haven't done it before or since. And I have no idea how I pulled that woman onto my bike so effortlessly."

"Wow." Emma gazed at her. Spellbound. Then, recovering, she said, "I only have one more question."

"Only one?"

Crystina had thousands.

"For now, yeah." Emma sighed wistfully. "Will you keep going? Will you keep listening? To the Spirit, I mean."

"Yes. Every day. Now that I've felt it—"

And just like last night and the night before, her mind's eye filled with a vision. This time in broad daylight. There was no mistaking it. The roads ignited in her mind, forming a path to a place she'd never been before. But somehow, she could see it.

"What's wrong?" Emma asked.

"I gotta go."

An urgency tugged on her soul and pulled her and her bike all the way back to the heart of Juniper City. In the thick of the traffic, it was impossible not to notice the attention she was attracting. People stopped in the street and hung out of car windows. Phone cameras flashed. Horns. Shouts. And then, a staggered applause from a table of customers at a sidewalk café. It was almost enough to distract her. But then the sirens blasted from an unmarked car making headway in her side mirrors. Red and blue lights flashed across its dash. Crystina *should* have stopped. A law-abiding citizen would have stopped. But there was a foreign rebellion stirring in her gut. So instead, she churned the throttle.

The unmarked car pursued her through the parting traffic. She knew they were there, but she no longer saw them in her mind. All she could see was a property with a barbwire fence. She had never been there before. But for some reason, the Lord was sending her there now.

Police motorbikes were next to join the pursuit, followed by two more cars and a helicopter. Anyone would think she was a criminal. Then again, maybe she was? She had ridden with a bare-headed passenger the other night and was now leading a pursuit.

A quiet still voice drowned out the sirens.

Keep going. Trust me.

Okay, Lord, I'm here. I'm trusting. Can I just please not get arrested? Please?

Cityscape turned to dust and dirt. A voice on the megaphone urged her to stop. She didn't. After all, her orders came from a Higher Power.

Crystina had reached forestry when she saw the dirt road. And she knew.

There.

Drifting around the corner, she raced toward the barbwire fence. Police followed.

Suddenly, a rifle cracked the air. She ducked and weaved. Bullets peppered the side of the unmarked car. All attention shifted to the property with its dingy trailer and aggressive canines.

Crystina shrank back and watched as more police approached. Stowing herself and her motorbike away in the nearby bushes, she watched with wide-eyed fascination.

"You're surrounded! Come out with your hands up!" the voice on the megaphone demanded.

She knew they were no longer talking to her. For the moment, she was forgotten. Instead, all attention was on the pony-tailed man in a tank top and jeans as he stumbled out of the trailer.

"Drop your weapon!" the voice on the megaphone demanded again.

The man did as he was told, and the police descended on him like ants. Crystina didn't even notice where half of them had come from, but suddenly the man was shoved into a police car in handcuffs, while a team of officers ventured inside.

An ambulance then arrived to attend to the woman being carried by one of the officers. Her head rested against his badged chest. Mascara streaked her face. Her ankles and wrists were bloodied.

Crystina released the breath she'd been holding. She was too intrigued to notice someone approach.

"You are quite the hero."

Crystina flinched and peered out from her hiding place.

"I apologize." The woman showed both hands followed by her badge. "I am Commander Kendra Woodhouse."

"Azure Blaze," she said with more confidence than she actually had.

The commander returned her badge to the inside of her vest. "Can I ask how you knew about this place?"

"I didn't."

Kendra stared at her with a fierce glare. "Then how did you lead us here?"

"The Holy Spirit."

Crystina had expected the commander to laugh but she didn't. Her brow creased as she stared long and hard into the tinted helmet screen.

Kendra stepped closer. "You mean, *God?*"

"The One and Only. Or Three in One, really."

"God *told* you to come here?"

"Just like He told me where to find that nurse."

Kendra exhaled loudly. "What is your name?"

"I already answered that."

"Well, do you know your license plates are illegible?"

"Don't worry, it's registered. But that's not what this whole pursuit has been about, has it?"

"Our team would like to know who you are," she said.

"Well, you can tell your team who I am. And tell them that I AM called me, and if they want me to keep doing my job then they'll ignore things like registration plates."

"You are asking us to ignore the law."

"No, just to focus on more important parts of upholding it."

"Well, either way, we have to know who we're working with," she said.

"Isn't it obvious?" She pointed to the sky.

"Then why doesn't He tell us Himself?"

"I don't know, Commander. Why do *you* think He called me to help you do your job?"

She silently studied her, and Crystina briefly wondered whether there was any chance of seeing through the dark tint of her helmet. Then again, if the

Lord had made her registration plates illegible to the naked eye, then He could disguise her as well.

"This is a crime scene," Kendra said sternly, "I suggest you go home."

CHAPTER 6

Confessions

"Let's go people!" Xavier clapped his hands to end yet another one of his scolding speeches to the marketing team. "Not *you*, Santos. My office. *Now*."

Crystina followed, hustling out of the boardroom, clipboard in hand, trying to keep pace. "Xavier, I actually need to leave on time today."

He didn't even flinch. "Well, it's either now or before work tomorrow but I'll need you to clear out your desk."

"I'm sorry?" She paused at the doorway to his office.

"Emma's article was waiting for me when I arrived this morning. It looks like she single-handedly saved you all. Or rather, *Azure Blaze* did. It'll be front page news tomorrow."

Her stomach flipped. "Okay, so why do I need to clear out my desk?"

"Because I need you to sit right *there*." He pointed to the workstation directly outside his corner office.

"I'm flattered, I really am, but..."

"So why do you have to leave on time today?" he asked in such a nonchalant way she was certain he didn't care about the answer.

"I have a new puppy and he is wreaking havoc at home," she said. "My poor Abuela..."

He lifted his head. "You live with your grandmother?"

"Ye-s."

"What about your parents?"

He clearly hadn't read her file very well. She swallowed hard and stated as matter-of-factly as she could, "My family died in an accident when I was six. Abuela and Papi raised me. Now it's just Abuela and I."

"Crystina, I had no idea."

It was the first time he had said her name.

"It's okay," she replied without thinking.

"No, it's not," he said as impulsively as hitting a ball across a court. "You never have to say those words to others, Crystina. You may say 'thank you', but never *it's okay*. Because it isn't and it never will be."

She stared at him. Wide-eyed and silent. Somehow, Amos Xavier had managed to perfectly articulate everything she had ever wanted to say in two understated words. She couldn't help but wonder why he was so versed in grief.

"So, let's try that again," he said. "Crystina, I am sorry for your loss."

He'd just called her Crystina three times in three minutes, and for the past three months he'd been calling her 'Santos'. She released a shaky breath and whispered, "Thank you."

He nodded once before returning his attention to his screen. "No child should grow up without a parent," he said, then added, "Now, go be a responsible pet owner."

She quietly backed away.

"Oh, and Santos?"

"Sir?"

"Make sure you're here early tomorrow. I want my new P.A. up and running by nine. I take my coffee black."

Her mouth split into a grin. "Good night, Xavier."

"Melchizedek dug up my tulips today," Abuela said the moment Crystina walked through the front door.

Crystina glanced sideways at his sweet face. He was a mixed breed to be sure, but in the light of day it was obvious he was predominantly German Shepherd. It was his caramel face and floppy ears that lent themselves to another breed.

"Well, I hope this cheers you up." She shrugged. "I got promoted today."

Abuela almost dropped dinner again. "What? Oh, my Crystina. What wonderful news!" She held her tightly. "We *needed* good news."

"Yes, yes, we did. Do you mind if I quickly call Jerry?"

"Of course, of course."

Crystina kissed Abuela's cheek, petted Chizzy's head, then rummaged for her phone. The subway had been too noisy to call, and she hadn't wanted to drop by unannounced again. But a quick call during his study time should be okay, right?

"Hey..."

"Hey you," she said brightly, "what are you up to?"

His voice reduced to a whisper. *"Just studying. You?"*

"Well, I have news but, are you in the library, can you talk?"

"Who are you talking to?" a feminine voice asked in the background.

And just like that, something sunk within her. "Oh, I'm sorry, it sounds like you're busy."

"Is that Crys?"

58

Her heart started to pound. "Is that *Harper?*"

Jeremiah groaned. *"Yes and yes, but it's not what either of you think... Crystina, what was your news?"*

"I got promoted to Amos Xavier's personal assistant," she said as loudly as she could. "It's a great opportunity. But I can hear that you're busy, so I'll let you go. Say hi to Harper for me."

And with that, she hit the red button on the touchscreen.

Abuela's concerned expression followed her all the way to the dining table. "Did that make you feel good?"

Her cheeks grew hot. She blinked away the sheen over her eyes.

Abuela took Crystina's hands and prayed over their meal. Just like Papi used to do, only he wasn't here anymore to do it. There were only the two of them now. Well, and Chizzy.

When Abuela was finished, Crystina asked in a small voice, "Is Chizzy really that bad behaved?"

A hint of a smile graced Abuela's face. "No. Of course not. But he did dig up my tulips. He's just bored."

"I'll take him out for a long walk tonight. Try to exhaust him." She forced a smile. "He's already looking fuller, don't you think? Not as skinny."

"Yes, I do think. I also think you are changing the subject." Abuela took a long sip of water. "Make sure you tell God about it. Whatever is going on in there." She waved her fork in the direction of Crystina's forehead before wielding it against her own dinner plate.

Crystina no longer felt hungry, but she ate for Abuela's sake. Once again, Abuela had cooked up a feast for them. She was so accustomed to cooking for a man. Now they'd be eating leftovers for days.

Once the beacon had been lit for the evening, Crystina fulfilled her promise and took Chizzy on a long walk through Juniper Bay. Something about having a dog by her side gave her confidence to walk alone. They had almost arrived in the old town when she was going to turn back, but in the distance, she saw St Peters. The house of worship seemed so out of place, like it was the ancient ruins of what was, and others simply built up around them. Iron, steel, and glass overshadowed it, but its ornate architecture and detailed stained-glass windows shone like a lamp in a dark place. According to the commemorative plaque by the gate, this late sixteenth century cathedral had been the first place of worship in Old Juniper—before the Earthquake claimed half of the city. Yet here stood a remnant of times long past. A sacred sanctuary. Holy ground.

As they approached, Crystina saw the Watchman sitting by the empty fountain amongst overgrown dry foliage. Chizzy bounded ahead, sniffing, and licking the priest.

"Sorry about him," she called.

The Watchman laughed. "Oh, that is quite alright. I am rather partial to animals. They seem to favor me in return."

His other worldliness intrigued her. She gestured to the stone bench where he sat. "May I?"

"Please. Who is your friend?"

"A bit of a stray. Like me, I guess."

"You are a daughter of God Almighty," he said with conviction and a fire in his eyes. "You could never be a stray."

She nodded silently.

"Why not let him play in the garden?" The Watchman shifted his weight to his walking aid as he rose. "It seems you need to talk."

"Like, confession?"

"If you like. Do you have something to confess?"

Crystina was ill-practiced at confession, Abuela was the professional in their shrinking family. Abuela was all for confession. Although she knew God forgave her sins, she took seriously the verse in James chapter five about confessing to one another. She had said God cleansed her, but the priest held a mirror for her to see herself clearly again.

Now, as Crystina sat in that tiny wooden space, there were no mirrors, only a kindly priest on the other side of the latticed screen.

"Forgive me," she began, "I have had sinful thoughts."

"We must take every thought captive to obey Christ," the Watchman said.

She knew this in theory, but it was easier said than done.

"But what if I continue to struggle?" she asked. "You see, there's this guy..."

CHAPTER 7

Just Like Him

Once Crystina had bared her soul to the Watchman, he prayed over her. He then left the conversation in the confessional box and walked her back to the garden, wielding his walking-aid down the narrow path round to the cemetery. The iron stokes of the fence were so far apart Chizzy had slipped through. The Watchman smiled to himself before using the gate.

"Melchizedek," he said firmly, "there will be no unearthing of bones today, thank you."

But Chizzy wasn't digging. He was listening, his ears pointed north.

"Chizzy?"

No sooner had his name left her lips, did her eyes drift closed and a vision reeled before her like a scene from a movie. It was no longer kept to her mind's eye. The Lord's direction was becoming more prominent.

"What is it?" the Watchman asked, his voice deep with concern.

When Crystina opened her eyes, she saw it clearly. "I gotta go."

She didn't hear his reply.

Chizzy leapt the fence as her feet rolled into a sprint. They raced across the overgrown garden and out onto the street. Chizzy's paws scratched the pavement as he met her supernatural pace. Pure clarity swept through her mind and they effortlessly ran three blocks.

"Help!" A woman's shrill scream pierced the cityscape. "Help! My baby..."

In the distance Crystina saw her. Running. Sobbing. Reaching out after a pair of red rear lights.

"What happened?" Crystina took hold of the woman's shoulder.

She writhed against her. "My baby... he stole my car... with my baby..."

Righteous anger burst in her soul and coursed through her body, kindling every part of her, bringing her awake. Alive. She had never felt so... alive.

"Jesus," she whispered, "if it is within Your will, please, give me the strength you gave *him*."

In that moment, she claimed the supernatural gift of speed given to the prophet of old. She propelled into the city traffic. Blurred lights streamed past. All she saw were the rear lights guiding her into narrow streets, deeper into the thick of Juniper City. Horns. Sirens. It all blurred together as she descended upon the car.

It was almost within reach.

And she felt like Elijah outracing the chariot on foot.

"Help me!" she screamed to the only One who could.

Then, with a strength not her own, Crystina launched herself forward. She pulled herself up by the spoiler as the driver began to lose control. Her only fear was for the baby inside. But what could she do? Hold on? How long for? Doubt crept into her mind and her hand started to slip.

"No." She gritted her teeth. "Not today." Fear and doubt could go to hell. God had not given her a spirit of fear but of power, love, and of a sound mind.

The car flailed but she reached for the handle of the back door and yanked it open. Her body was guided inside. It wasn't her. It couldn't have been her. No, her body was not its own. She settled one hand on the screaming infant while she leant forward with the other and pulled up the handbrake. The car slid. Drifting. The driver banged his head on the window glass. Her arms clung to the car seat, and she leaned, trying to shield the baby with as much of her body as possible. The car slid to a halt. No collision. No oncoming traffic or injured pedestrians. It was a pure miracle. God's grace covered them so completely. And the continual cry of that infant was bittersweet for Crystina's soul. This innocent child, so terrified. But, *alive*.

More sirens.

Crystina breathed slowly. She could smell blood, but it wasn't coming from the baby. *Thank you, Jesus.* That was when she noticed the snowflake fracture in the window beside the car seat, the window her own head had evidently collided with.

Once the adrenaline wore off, the throbbing came into focus. Sharp pain settled in as Crystina noticed the blood dripping down her face.

The car tore open with police, medics, and one hysterical mother.

Crystina breathed deep.

A medic tentatively felt the infant's neck while the car seat was still in the car. For what must have seemed like an eternity for the mother, the medic continued to check over the baby before releasing the car seat and lifting it from the back seat. Police escorted the stretcher with the thieving driver. Then Crystina peered out into the balmy night. Her appearance was met by applause.

News crews loomed beyond the crowd, but the police kept them at bay. Though, she must have been barely recognizable with all the blood.

"It's not as bad as it looks," she said softly.

"Regardless, we'll be giving you a thorough look over," a medic said.

"If you could just clean me up, I'm honestly fine." Crystina looked up and into the face of an awe-struck woman.

"I know that voice," she said in hushed tones.

"You're that nurse!" Crystina blinked up at her, wincing as the blood stung her eyes. "I mean, I, um, saw you in the um... news... argh." Crystina smeared blood away from her forehead.

"Come with me," the woman said gently, leading Crystina into the back of an ambulance. Chizzy swiftly followed, leaping up into the van. The medic closed the doors on the camera flashes and prying eyes. She then turned and gazed at Crystina, her eyes brimming with respect and hope. "I know it's you."

Crystina swallowed hard.

"As you can see, I've had a shift in career since the attack." She started to rummage through her kit, pulling out antiseptic and gauze. "We usually don't allow pets in the back but, for you, we can make an exception."

Chizzy set himself by Crystina's feet as she rested on the stretcher.

The woman approached with her findings. "Now, this may sting a little."

Crystina nodded and braced herself. She remained silent until something glinted at her from around the nurse's neck. A crucifix glimmered in the fluorescent lighting.

"Are you allowed to wear that?"

"My cross? Well, no one has told me not to. Since that night, I haven't taken it off."

"You're a Christian?"

"I am." Tentatively, she padded the cut. "I'm Laura, by the way."

"I'm—"

"Azure Blaze," Laura cut in, then shook her head. "If I don't know, then I won't have to lie."

Crystina smiled.

"Well, Azure Blaze, you're all sorted. I would send you in for observations, but something tells me you'd rather rest at home. So where can I take you?"

"Juniper Bay? If the news crews don't follow."

"I think the cops have them under control for now. Let's go."

When Crystina arrived at the lighthouse, she was met at the front door.

Abuela's hands flew to her mouth and she gasped. "So, it's true!"

"I'm okay, Abuela."

She took hold of Crystina's hand, leading her into the kitchen where the television set was blaring.

"She saved my baby!" the mother cried. "You should have seen her. It was incredible. The Lord gave her the speed of Elijah!"

Breath caught in Crystina's chest.

The next clip showed Laura, still a little bloodied from their encounter. Her fingers subtly touched the cross that hung around her neck. "Yes, it was Azure Blaze who saved the infant. I recognized her voice instantly."

"Do you know her identity?" the reporter prodded.

"No," Laura answered honestly, "I do not."

Crystina staggered back and slumped into a dining chair. "They are both Christians," she said, breathless.

Tears streamed down Abuela's face. "And God sent you, my beloved granddaughter, to rescue them."

She reached down to scratch Chizzy between the ears. She needed to hold onto something tangible. This was all so strange. "So, this whole Azure Blaze thing, is to protect God's people? His daughters? I wonder if the woman in the trailer..." The pain began to pulsate again, and she groaned.

"*God* will protect God's people," Abuela said. "Do not put that pressure on yourself. But you are His *vessel*. Continue to listen to Him. Let Him guide you always."

"I'm trying."

"I know you are." Abuela kissed her hair. "I know. I also know this isn't an easy calling. Especially in a time of so much confusion."

She peered up. "Oh?"

A slight smile curled Abuela's mouth. "Jeremiah is waiting upstairs."

"In the lantern room?"

"No, in your bedroom. I thought it would be more comfortable."

Her insides plummeted. "Oh!" Suddenly, she wasn't Azure Blaze. She was little Crystina Santos who hadn't cleaned her room before her best friend came to visit.

She half expected Chizzy to follow her as she raced for the spiral staircase, but he knew who filled his food bowl and she was dotingly petting him and praising him for looking after her granddaughter.

When Crystina arrived at the doorway to her bedroom, she noticed Abuela had already been in and tidied—she could have mentioned that.

Breathless and a little dizzy, she mustered a small, "Hey."

Jeremiah looked up from the desk by the window before leaping to his feet. "Are you okay?" He closed the space between them in a few strides, his gaze fixed on her forehead.

"It looks worse than it is." She curled her legs beneath her as she plonked down on the bed. "It's late. Don't you have to study?"

He sat down opposite her on the bed. "Yeah, but I wanted to talk to you about Harper."

Crystina had forgotten. In all the adrenaline, her 'guy' problems had slipped to the back of her mind. "Oh, yeah."

His brow furrowed. "You don't care?"

"If you're happy, I'm happy."

Jeremiah's eyes narrowed. "Really?"

"Really," she lied. Happy was going a bit far. But Crystina could appreciate his happiness, from a distance. "Of course, how *she* could make you happy, I don't think I could ever understand. But to each their own."

His mouth twitched. "Can't you just admit the idea bothers you?"

She gently rubbed the patch on her forehead. She wasn't up for this conversation. "It bothers me that she ditched us senior year and now she ignores me but apparently wants to date you."

He glanced out the window then back to her. "Why does it surprise you that she wants to date me?"

Crystina licked her lips to keep them from drying out. Where was this coming from?

"Just because *you* don't want to date me, doesn't mean I'm not a catch." He shrugged, as though confirming a decision she had already made. Only, she hadn't. She just knew what happened to people she loved. And so, there would always have to be a barrier between Jeremiah and her. For *his* sake.

"I can't date anyone," she said softly, "least of all you."

He was up off the bed and at her door in three seconds flat.

"Wait." She rubbed her forehead again, wincing. "That didn't come out right."

"I think you were pretty clear, Crystina." He met her eye. "But just so you know, I have zero interest in Harper Lloyd."

She shut her eyes tight, praying the conversation would end. She couldn't do this now.

"I had zero interest in her in high school when she offered to pay for my ticket to the formal," he went on. "Because I had zero interest in going without you, and our scholarships didn't cover it. *That*'s why she ditched us. But even now, she wanted to talk. And I had—"

"Zero interest?" she offered.

"Well, yeah."

Talk about information overload. She was drowning in it. And none of it made much sense. "That's a whole lot of, or well, lack of interest going on..." she muttered, unable to string a cohesive thought.

He stepped toward her. "Crys, are you okay?"

"Mm? Of course, I'm..."

Then everything went black.

CHAPTER 8

Personal Convictions

"Santos, if you didn't want the position, you could have just said so."

Lights flickered as Crystina attempted to focus on the figure before her. She knew she was in her bedroom. But she also knew *he* shouldn't have been.

Wincing, she struggled to sit up. "My head hurts."

"You have what the nurse called a delayed concussion," Xavier said matter-of-factly.

"The nurse?"

"Your grandmother."

"Oh, Abuela, of course. She used to be a, um, nur—" She rubbed her forehead. "Sorry, what are you doing here?"

"Your *Abuela* called the office for you, to let someone know you wouldn't be coming in."

She peered up at him as he loomed over her bed dressed in his usual business attire. "That doesn't answer my question."

"I'm a sceptic, Santos." He shrugged. "I had to see for myself."

"You check on all your employees?"

"I had business this way. I thought I'd drop in."

She was so confused. "You had business in Juniper Bay?"

"Look at you, already feeling better. You know where you are, *and* how to make a guest feel unwelcome. Congratulations." His tone was saturated in sarcasm before he added, "I brought flowers if that helps."

Her focus leapt to the bouquet on the desk so fast it made her head spin. "Oh."

"You're welcome."

"You didn't have to do that."

"I know, you're welcome." He turned to leave. "See you tomorrow, Santos. Early. Don't forget."

"Yes, sir."

"And make sure you catch up on our exclusive when you're up to reading."

She inwardly groaned. "Yes, sir."

"Xavier," he corrected, pausing at her bedroom door. "And try not to fall down any more stairs."

She nodded silently but continued to stare after him until Abuela appeared in the doorway.

"Jeremiah was here but I sent him home." Abuela set a mug of steaming tea on the bedside table. "Beautiful flowers."

Crystina's eyes narrowed. "They're *unusual*."

Abuela followed her critical stare. "Delphiniums. Strangely, they were your mother's favorite. She liked that they were naturally—"

"*Blue*." Her eyes grew round. "Abuela, did you tell Xavier I fell down the stairs?"

"No," she replied, horrified at the thought. "I said it was a car accident. I wasn't going to *lie*."

Crystina's heart thudded. It was all she could hear. If she didn't already have a headache, she was sure it would've started pounding along too.

"What's wrong?" Abuela asked.

Crystina couldn't tear her eyes away from the floral bouquet. "He knows."

The following morning Crystina read from Psalm 18. Her focus danced over the words until it landed on verse 28—*For You will light my lamp; The LORD my God will enlighten my darkness.* As the words washed over her, she fell to her knees and stayed there beside the bed until her body ached for release.

Dawn touched the horizon. She wasn't sure how long she'd been there. But with all the sleep she'd gained with her concussion, she felt prepared for whatever this day would bring. Because Jesus was already there.

She arrived at the office early as promised and quietly moved her limited belongings from the cramped grey desk with its curved dividers, to the stately matt-white station outside Amos Xavier's corner office. He had already organized a plaque for her.

Crystina Santos, Personal Assistant.

She rested a Bible in the top drawer—a practice she did at her own desk for as long as she could remember—then she added the finishing touches. Though, it still looked bare. She really couldn't understand how Xavier trusted her with such an immaculate surface.

"And how are we feeling this morning?" he asked, placing an extra-large takeaway coffee on her desk.

Crystina glanced at the clock and rose to meet his eyes. "It's only eight a.m. I would've had coffee for you at nine."

He leaned over the desk. "You can just say *thank you.*"

"Thank you," she responded quickly, reaching for the cup.

"I took a wild guess."

She watched him enter his office before taking her first sip. It was nutty. And strong. Hazelnut latte? She licked her lips. She wasn't usually one for spoiling herself with anything fancier than instant coffee, but she could get used to this.

Crystina turned her attention to the screen. *The exclusive.* She had almost forgotten. She logged in to the Legion International Media desktop app and scrolled until she reached the full article. She didn't want to get distracted by the fact that her newly appointed title was splashed all over the front page, calling her a 'superhero'. In the article, Emma had faithfully quoted her word for word.

Crystina smiled to herself as she read Emma's humble description of the heroine of Juniper City, and how 'Azure Blaze' had credited all foreknowledge and ability to God. Which begged the question, did the reader believe there was a God? There, Emma left the article like a cliff hanger. And Crystina was shocked it was allowed to go to print.

"What do you think?" Xavier asked. "Did she do it justice?"

She flinched. "You scared me."

"Well?"

"It's... *bold.*"

"It's right up your alley though, right? With the whole God thing."

Her eyes narrowed slightly as she peered up at him. "Well, what do *you* think of it?"

"Personally, I'm an atheist. But in our current socioeconomic climate, it sells." He shrugged. "That's all that matters."

"That's really all you care about?"

"It's my job, Santos."

"I thought you said you had a life?"

"Touché." His brows rose, in amusement more than offence, a wry smile igniting his pale eyes. "Do you think Azure Blaze will trust Legion International Media with future exclusives?"

She sat a little straighter in her chair. "I'm not sure."

With a suave turn on his heel, he returned to his office. No authoritative march. No condescending remarks. Only a brief but completely professional request for her to hold all his calls.

Crystina quickly discovered being Amos Xavier's personal assistant focused primarily on the *personal* aspect. When she wasn't answering his calls, she ran errands and fetched his dry cleaning, a green smoothie, or more caffeine. He didn't eat much. She didn't ask why. But she was determined his lack of appetite wouldn't steal hers.

When hunger finally led her to the border of aggravation, she directed his calls to voicemail and popped her head into his office. However, with a single disapproving look, Xavier silenced her before she even began to speak.

"I have a lunch meeting," he said.

It was two p.m.

"Great. I've already diverted the phone so I can—"

"You're coming with me."

"Excuse me?"

"I need someone to take notes," he said, closing his desk drawer and locking it with a key from his bulging set. "Unless, you have something more important to do?"

The European in her certainly could have argued the importance of food, and it probably would've involved the use of her hands. But she figured since she had yesterday off sick, she should try to be as agreeable as possible.

"There are worse ways to spend a Friday afternoon," he said, leading the way out of his office and into the hallway. "Come on."

With her notebook in one hand and purse in the other, Crystina followed down the quiet office hallway to the open plan space lined with divided desks. He practically paraded her past the junior assistants. Harper's laser focus didn't shift from her screen. But it didn't matter. There was only one person Crystina was interested in seeing, in giving her a small pat well done on the way past. Only, Emma wasn't among them.

"Where's Emma?" Crystina asked in hushed tones.

"You're so out of the loop, Santos." He pressed the elevator button and waited. "She has been moved upstairs to the journalism department."

"What?" she squealed. A little too loudly.

Taken aback, Xavier smiled. Broad and brilliant.

"Uh, sorry." She returned to her hushed tones as they slipped into the elevator. "That's so exciting."

His smile faded but the spark in his eyes remained. "Well, she has proven herself to be very resourceful. Besides, she seems to be the only one who has been able to get Azure Blaze to talk. And in case you haven't noticed, she's kind of big news right now."

"And she sells."

He nodded once. "She sells."

"And that's what you care about, because it's your job."

"Exactly."

The doors shuddered closed, and Crystina held her notebook and purse to her chest, smiling to herself.

"Okay, I'll bite, why is it so exciting?" Xavier asked.

"She wants to be a journalist," she said, thinking the answer was obvious. "It's her dream. This is amazing. You made my day."

His Adam's apple bounced in his throat, and he stared at the closed steel doors. When they finally reopened on the ground floor, he blinked as though coming to. "My car's out front."

Crystina wasn't sure what she had expected, but she hadn't expected *this.* A slightly beat-up silver sedan was parked up against the curb. She half expected Xavier to announce that it was a joke, and he would proceed to call for his car, or to press the unlock button so a Lamborghini would beep. But no. He opened the passenger door for her before making his way around the bonnet to the driver's side. This car just didn't suit Amos Xavier, Editor-in-Chief.

A short comfortable silence unfolded as they drove through the backstreets of Juniper City and Xavier pulled into an almost invisible undercover carpark.

"Where are we?" she asked.

Xavier turned on the headlights. "In the basement of JCPD."

"O-kay. But why?"

He pulled into a car space marked 'Guest' and cut the engine. "Santos, once our exclusive went to print, I received a call from the commander here demanding to know our source."

"And?"

His eyebrows rose. "Are you really going to make me say it?"

"This isn't a lunch meeting, is it?"

"No. In fact it's not even my meeting," he said. "It's yours."

"So, *you're* here, because..."

"I suppose you could call me your chaperone," he said, clearly unimpressed with the title. "Also, my father is supposedly on the board of the department, so there's a distant connection there—*very* distant—but it has been exploited nonetheless."

"I take it you don't have much to do with your dad?"

"He didn't have time for me. So now I don't have time for him. End of story."

Crystina knew better than to press the matter. "Well, do you know what the *department* wants?"

He bit his lip and stared blankly ahead. "They want to speak to Azure Blaze. I guess they need a little help from the big man upstairs."

"You don't even believe He exists."

"I don't. But they do. Or at least, *she* does. The commander that is. She seems to think your 'gift' is genuine."

"And you don't?"

Crystina made the mistake of meeting his gaze. Xavier studied her, as though she was some abstract piece of art.

She turned to the window. "So, I'm going in alone?"

"You've always got God, right?" He chuckled. "Just head up those stairs. Someone will direct you, I'm sure."

CHAPTER 9

Always + Forever

The officer on reception led Crystina deep within the labyrinth of Juniper City Police Department Headquarters to a sterile office. She was met by a familiar pair of fierce eyes.

Commander Kendra Woodhouse peered up from a heavy manilla file. Masses of curly dark hair framed her deep-bronze face as she stared at Crystina. She seemed unimpressed.

"We have a situation," Kendra began before Crystina had even sat down. "It is strictly confidential."

Crystina floundered into the seat opposite before she found her voice. "It'll stay between me and, well, *Him*." She pointed to the ceiling.

Kendra's body visibly relaxed but an intensity still burned in her expression "Regardless of your *connections*, we first need to ensure you'll be able to take care of yourself in the field. You can't become a liability while assisting us."

Crystina blinked up at her.

"You often put yourself in compromising situations," Kendra explained.

"I don't mean to. I'm just called to them."

"Well, this calling has led you into danger," she went on. "And if this is a foreshadow of things to come, we need you to be prepared."

"What do you mean?"

"The department would like to put you through some self-defense training. Nothing too strenuous. Just educate you enough to hold your own out there."

"But I'm not a violent person."

"Azure Blaze," Kendra began again, this time more gently. "I know this may feel conflicting for you, so I would encourage you to pray about it. But remember, there are many times God calls His people into battle in the Bible. We are not asking you to go against your beliefs. But neither can we have you involved in a case if you are unprepared."

Something had shifted. Now Kendra was looking at her like she was some sort of divine oracle. She wasn't. Clearly. And Crystina reminded her of that the moment Kendra opened her mouth to speak again.

"I can't guarantee anything," she said, before Kendra could get another word out. "Whatever it is, I can't guarantee God will speak to me. This isn't a Joseph or Daniel situation. I'm just *me*."

"Well, *just you*," she said, "we know you can't make any promises. But, since we're being honest, I will level with you. You're our last hope."

Crystina swallowed hard.

"Here, take this." Kendra slid a smart phone across the desk. "You'll find my direct number in contacts, should you decide to assist us."

"I'll pray about it, Commander," Crystina said.

"Good." Her voice was deep, sure, and strong. "And you can call me Kendra."

"Thank goodness it's Friday." Crystina slumped into Xavier's passenger seat once the 'lunch meeting' had ended.

"Let's get you home," he said simply and started the engine.

"Only if it's not too much trouble." She shrugged. "Otherwise, I can take the subway from work, I wouldn't want you to—"

"Santos. Stop talking."

Smiling, she turned her attention to the cityscape and watched the scenes change out of the passenger window until the water came into view. A shiver ran down her spine and all amusement fell away. Would the memories never fade? At night she could barely see the water as she rode Papi's motorbike or walked or sat in the lantern room, but in the harsh light of the day she saw the waves crash against the rocks and couldn't help but wonder who they'd steal from her next.

"Your boyfriend's here," Xavier said, ducking slightly to look beyond the sun visor.

Jeremiah reclined on a rug on the patch of grass, reading a heavy book with Chizzy beside him. He lowered it slightly when the car neared and Chizzy's tail started to wag.

Crystina knew she should have corrected Xavier but part of her didn't want to. So, she thanked him again for the ride, collected her purse and notebook, and made short work of leaving his car. When Jeremiah stood to greet her, Crystina let her belongings drop to the ground to hug him.

His strong arms tightened around her, and he lifted her so her feet no longer touched the ground. The past week melted away as she breathed him in. Soap, fresh laundry, and a hint of Old Spice.

"He's gone," he whispered into her hair.

"I know, I just wanted to hug you."

He placed her back down.

She playfully nudged him. "*What?*"

"Nothin'." He stepped back. "How was your day?"

"Interesting," she replied, her eyes widening for emphasis. "I'll tell you and Abuela over dinner."

His pace slowed. "Sorry, I can't stay. I've gotta study."

"Then, why are you here now?"

"I wanted to make sure you were okay." He shrugged. "And now I have."

"Oh." She paused by the front door. "So, you're really not coming in?"

Chizzy bounded past them at the sound of Abuela scraping the dog food can with a spoon.

"No, but he is." Jeremiah flashed his lopsided grin. "But hey, tomorrow. Let's hang. Make the most of your weekend now you're a responsible adult who works nine to five."

She leaned her wounded head against the door frame. "I don't know about that last part but hanging out sounds great."

He nodded once. "Get some rest, okay?"

"Mm-kay."

"Promise? Best friends keep promises, remember?"

She beamed. "Always and forever."

When Crystina and Abuela sat down for dinner, they both bowed their heads, folded their hands, and closed their eyes. Then they both waited. Silence. Even Chizzy, who had already devoured his food, shared in the reverent moment from the living room rug. Crystina peeked up, glancing from Abuela to Papi's empty chair. This was how it was going to be now.

"Our Father in heaven," she began softly and watched as tears slid down Abuela's worn cheeks. "Hallowed be Your name. Your Kingdom come. Your will be done on earth as it is in heaven..."

Abuela began to whisper along.

"Give us this day our daily bread. And forgive us our debts, as we forgive our debtors. And do not lead us into temptation, but deliver us from the evil one. For Yours is the kingdom and the power and the glory forever. Amen."

Crystina wanted to tell Abuela all about her day. But now was not the time. So they both pushed food around their plates until enough time had passed. Abuela claimed tiredness and escaped to her bedroom. Crystina then carried her Bible and journal, a thermos of tea, and her phone all the way to the top of the spiral staircase. As she passed Abuela's bedroom on the second floor, weeping seeped from behind the door. Through a crack of golden light in the doorway, she saw Abuela on her knees by her bed, the Word of God open on the quilt, her face pressed to the open page. This was life now. Pressing into Jesus as much as they could. The brokenness of the world had stood still for them for a season, allowing Abuela and Papi to watch Crystina grow into a young woman. Something her parents and three older brothers would never get to do. Then, Papi said goodbye. Silently.

Now it was her responsibility to man the lighthouse, to ignite the beacon each night. Only in winter, when the bay froze over, had Papi rested from his duties. Winter was dark in Juniper Bay. Far darker than the city with all its lights and infrastructure. But winter was still months away. It was the middle of summer, which meant as each evening descended upon Juniper Bay, Crystina set to work. Then as the light rotated around and beyond, she sat and watched the constellations above come and go. Come with the dark. Go with the light. She sipped her tea, and opened her Bible, ready to listen. Unlike the silence of the dining room table, this one was filled with reverence and beauty.

Until, rather unceremoniously, her phone chimed.

"*You awake?*" it read.

Jeremiah.

Her thumbs quickly responded. "*Yes. I'm in the lantern room. Shouldn't you be studying?*"

"*I'm too distracted. Looking forward to tomorrow.*"

She smiled to herself. "*Oh really? Why's that?*"

"*Very funny... I get to hang out with my best friend for the first time in forever.*"

For some reason, seeing the word 'friend' in black and white text stung. It shouldn't have. But it did. *"So what's the plan?"*

"How about I pick you up early? Did you want to bring Chizzy?"

"I think I'd prefer him to stay so Abuela isn't alone."

There was a long pause. *"Am I being selfish taking you out tomorrow?"*

Her brow furrowed as she stared long and hard at the question, then slowly typed, *"If you are, then I'm being selfish for wanting to go out with you."*

As soon as she had pressed 'send', she reread the sentence in horror. *Go out* with him? Would he think she was insinuating something? His mom had been right all that time ago. Things would change between them. They couldn't stay children forever. Why did it have to be so complicated that her feelings even came out subliminally? *Lord, what do I do? How do I act normal around him tomorrow? When I can't stop watching him... and... smelling him...*

She should suggest they do something that gave him B.O. But what? Anything physical to make sure she couldn't detect that soap, fresh linen, and that hint of Old Spice. She blushed. Knowing him, he'd probably look even more striking with bright eyes from exercise and sweaty sheen over his biceps. She shook her head. She had to be careful. If only he could see her now with her cheeks ablaze. He'd know without a doubt. And she'd risk losing one of the most important people in her life. Again.

"How about a picnic? We have leftover pizza."

Crystina sighed. Maybe they could hike to the picnic spot? But it would only work if he promised to look and smell terrible. She chuckled to herself and replied simply, *"Sounds great."*

"Awesome. See you bright and early!"

She grinned. He was such a morning person. *"I'll be ready."*

"Goodnight. Love you. Always + forever."

Her cheeks burned. They had always used *that* word. Always told each other they loved each other. Only, in person, they'd always said, "Love *ya.*" As if the second word was thrown tactlessly across a room. It was an affectionate tag they would use when going separate ways. "Love *ya.*" Crystina might blow a throw away kiss. Jeremiah might leap to catch it then slap it on his cheek. It was all innocent. They'd done it for years.

But that wasn't a little word caught on the wind.

It was a very distinct –

You.

How could she respond to that? Maybe he was just being extra nice considering the past week. It had been rough, he probably just wanted her to know he was there for her despite it all. But Crystina always thought an "I love you, *too*" was a copout. It was replying, it wasn't declaring.

She cleared her throat and replied with exclamation points to prove she was fine, excited for tomorrow, and not at all afraid to tell him she loved him. Not in the least afraid.

"And I love you, Jerry! Always + forever. Sweet dreams!"

Then he sent something she didn't expect. *"When you lie down, you will not be afraid; Yes, you will lie down and your sleep will be sweet. Prov. 3:24 x"*

And just like that, Crystina couldn't wait for tomorrow to come.

CHAPTER 10

No Going Back

"When I was a child, I talked like a child, I thought like a child, I reasoned like a child. When I became a man, I put the ways of childhood behind me."
1 CORINTHIANS 13:11

Gravel crunched beneath the tires of Jeremiah's old Buick as he pulled up outside the lighthouse. He half expected he'd have to wait, maybe even head upstairs and wake sleeping beauty. But to his surprise, the front door shuddered open to reveal a bright and very much awake Crystina in a white linen sundress.

His heart almost stopped completely.

"Hey, hey," she chimed as she slid into the front seat, settling her aviator sunglasses in place.

"Well, good morning, sunshine." He beamed and pulled back onto the road. He wasn't sure where her joy had come from, but it was contagious. He glanced sideways, watching her relax into the seat, her wounded head leaning back against the rest. He clenched his teeth and his jaw pulsed. It was going to be a good day.

"Oh, I love this song!" She reached for the dial and turned the volume up. He cringed as she began to sing along. But she spied him. "Come on then, maestro. You show me how it's done."

He chuckled. "I don't know this one."

"Well, you'll just have to put up with my tone-deaf singing then."

It was a small price to pay to see her smile.

He briefly wondered if he should ask about Abuela or her week at work or whether the Holy Spirit had called her to another situation. He likely knew the answer to the last one. It would've been all over the news. But the silence was comfortable. Well, *his* silence. She was still crooning.

"So, where are we going?" she asked at last.

"It's a surprise."

"Just so long as it's somewhere I can go in this dress. I'm probably not up for mountain climbing to the perfect cliff-face picnic spot."

He glanced at her slender fingers tapping along to the beat of the music—he wanted to hold that hand. He wanted to watch as their fingers wove together.

Tangled. Black and white. Well, caramel. The white dress offset her subtle Hispanic complexion and, as she relaxed in the passenger seat of his car, she glowed.

"What?" she asked, catching him in one of his lingering glances. Her face then split into a grin. "You should be watching the road!"

"I am." He laughed. "This is just... nice."

"Yeah, it is." She reached over and gave his hand a squeeze. But as she went to retract it, Jeremiah did what his daring heart desired. He held on. And he gripped the steering wheel with the other all the harder.

Suddenly, there was a shift.

Crystina sat a little straighter and her carefree singing came to a swift end. She wiggled her fingers slightly, as though getting comfortable within his as their hands rested together by the gear stick. Jeremiah was careful to keep his lopsided grin concealed on the side of his face she couldn't see, then bit his lip to keep it from spreading. Then he caught a flash of her dimple as she turned to face the window. Maybe, just maybe, this wasn't all in his imagination. Maybe something *had* changed between them? And for the first time he allowed himself to pray the words he'd been holding back for so long. *Please, Jesus. Let her be falling in love with me too.*

The comfortable silence became weighted with anticipation as they headed into the mountains beyond Juniper. Part of Jeremiah couldn't wait to explore their destination with Crystina and the other part of him just wanted to keep driving like this. Hand in hand.

Jeremiah turned the car into the conservation park set in the thick of the rainforest's lush foliage. "So..."

"Yeah?"

He gave her hand a small squeeze. "You're okay?"

He didn't know what he was asking. Was he asking about Papi? Or Abuela? Or work? Or Azure Blaze? Or was he seeking confirmation that the past forty-minutes of hand-holding had set off fireworks in her stomach too?

Crystina folded her sunglasses and left them on the dashboard. "I will be." She rolled her head to face him. "But this place is the perfect distraction, thank you."

Reluctantly, he released her hand to undo his seatbelt. "No cliffs, I promise."

"Okay, let's do this."

Jeremiah carried the picnic basket and rug, leading the way down the narrow path like wooden-bridges that wove through moss-covered trees and rock with vines hanging overhead. Crystina followed close behind but kept her hands to herself as she carried the thermos. He led her to where the trees thinned and a small off-the-trail marsh led to a body of water at the base of a roaring waterfall.

Crystina stopped in her tracks.

He paused, gazing back at her. "Remember the first time we went swimming after the accident?"

Her face drained white.

"Well, I thought you might need a bit of a crazy trust exercise again."

"Jerry, I know you're trying to help..."

He rested the basket and rug on the grass and held his hand out for her. "It's okay. Remember that night? How much better you felt?"

Her eyes drifted closed for a moment and he wondered if he had done the right thing bringing her here. Or if he was about to ruin everything.

She sighed. "I remember..."

"Well?"

She leaned down to rest the thermos on the ground. "You better not let go of me for a *second*."

"Never."

She took hold of his hand and it felt like home. Sure, once upon a time they had swum as kids in Juniper Bay. Then as they grew older, Dad had baptized them both in those waters. Then Dad lost his battle to cancer, and they hadn't swum together since. Last summer they had intended to, but with so much time passed, Crystina backed out. So they had just sat on the sand in their bathing suits, talking about their plans after senior year. Of course, it hadn't looked like this. For starters, they were both supposed to be at JCU. Second of all, *Crystina* hadn't looked like this. Or had she? Had he just been too close to notice?

He gulped as she waded in. She was fully clothed, but her dress clung to her the moment it touched the water. He quickly took off his t-shirt and went in after her in his shorts.

She turned. "You let go!"

"Just to take my shirt off." He raised his hands in defense before offering one to her.

He watched her eyes shift ever so briefly, from his chest to his face to his hand. She took it and held on tight.

"You ready?" he asked.

She released a shaky breath. "As I'll ever be, I guess."

"I won't let you go. Not for a second."

He lowered himself into the water and gently tugged her hand. She climbed onto his back the way she used to do when they were kids, when the waves set off her panic attacks and the very idea of the ocean induced night terrors. But here, the water was still except for the slight ripples from the far-off waterfall. Her arms wrapped around his neck as he kicked off from the bank, gliding through the crystal water. She held onto his body. Hers slightly cool against his warmth. He took large breaths above the surface then exhaled underwater as he swam. She once said that her only comfort in the water was knowing he was a strong swimmer.

"There're some caverns up ahead," he nodded, floating in the water for a moment. "Wanna go?"

"Okay," she whispered against his ear.

He'd almost forgotten how close she was. Not anymore though. He could feel her breath on his neck. Jeremiah led her into the wide-open mouth of the first cave, the swirling of the water echoed off the jagged walls. He followed the caves deeper and felt her arms tighten around him.

"We can turn back anytime," he said softly.

"I know," she whispered. "I'm okay."

"Good. Because we're almost at the best part."

He swam closer and closer into the darkness until the light could barely be seen. But above them, on the roof of the deepest cavern, shone a constellation of green.

"Wow," Crystina breathed.

"Glow worms." Jeremiah held onto her small arms as he steadied himself to float upright in the water, kicking his legs.

She hung on his back. "It's beautiful."

He glanced over his shoulder. *She* was beautiful.

"What?" she whispered again.

He craned his neck back to meet her gaze. "Nothin'."

Her wide brown eyes stared back at him. Frozen. He could see the confusion written on her face. He knew it well because it was the same conflict he was battling. If he dared to cross the line and stray beyond the boundaries of friendship, things would never be the same again. Everything would change. Was he really prepared for that? Even if she wanted him the way he wanted her, would it last? They had a good thing. They were almost a part of each other's families. Once upon a time, they practically lived under the same roof, alternating between the roofs, of course. If he took one more step, leaned in ever so slightly, she would know. And she would know that *he* would know that she would know. This game they'd been playing would self-destruct.

"So, why did you see Harper the other day?" she asked softly, as though not to disturb the worms.

Of all the things she wanted to talk about. Harper? Really?

"She showed up at my house."

"Well, that was very... presumptuous."

He chuckled, maneuvering himself to face her. Though, not letting go of her. Not for a second. "Mom let her in. I never got around to explaining the whole situation to her, so she just treated Harper like a long-lost daughter or something."

"Oh." Frown lines formed on Crystina's face. "So what did she want?"

"To apologize, would you believe it. For putting me in an awkward position last year."

"Really?"

"Yes, really," he said softly, suddenly distracted by her scent.

She cleared her throat. "Well, what did you say?"

"I told her it's all in the past and that I forgive her."

"And?"

"And she asked me to go out for coffee with her," he said.

Her mouth gaped. "Did you?"

"No, Crystina." He grinned. "No, I didn't. I said it was all in the past and that's where it should stay."

"Oh."

Jeremiah stared up into Crystina's face as she floated, arms draped around him. "So, is this still okay? Not too scary?"

"Define scary..."

Again, he thought his heart had stopped. Was he still breathing? He hoped so. For a long moment, they simply floated, her words hanging in the air between them. He wondered what it would be like to close that space. To show her what she really meant to him. To admit that he was undeniably in love with his best friend and no amount of prayer against it had worked. He wondered what it would be like to kiss Crystina.

He was about to shift so she could climb on his back again. He was about to return to the safety of the game, ignore the tension and just hold onto childhood memories as though it would keep them from making a terrible mistake. But he didn't. Instead, he gripped her arms. But no sooner did he pull her in did she break away, pressing against his shoulders, keeping him at arm's length.

"We should go," she said swiftly. "The tea will get cold."

"Yeah. Yeah, of course."

Jeremiah couldn't bring himself to admit how he ached for her and longed to hold her closer, to protect her and love her. Love her the way Christ loved His church. But just like He had to give up so much for His love, so too it seemed would Jeremiah.

He maneuvered himself so she could settle onto his back, and he swam toward the sunlight, leaving behind the intimacy of the cavern. Leaving behind the moment he almost kissed her.

She was rigid on his back. And he knew it wasn't the water that had frightened her this time. The game was up. Because she would know that *he* knew that she knew. So that even without the kiss, there was no going back.

CHAPTER 11

The Common Thread

Crystina didn't know what to think. Part of her was angry at Jeremiah. He had ruined everything she had been fighting so hard to preserve. Almost a year had gone by since he'd started at JCU and in that time she'd barely seen him. She had been working casual jobs here and there before her position at Legion International Media, so it wasn't her fault. She was available. He was just too busy for her. And in that time, he could have had who knew how many girlfriends she wasn't aware of.

But that night, when the Holy Spirit called her to the old bridge, she knew he was the first person she wanted to tell. A text message just wouldn't have sufficed. She was tired of the black and white friendship of their phones. She wanted to see him. She wanted to share that moment with him.

What Crystina hadn't expected was for him to be so markedly changed. He wasn't a boy anymore. He was a man. And if she was honest, that scared her. Because suddenly, she couldn't see past the handsome man at the window to the lanky best mate who had dared her to eat chicken feet in the food court at Chinatown then proceeded to walk the deep-fried claws across the table. No, all the nuances of their childhood had faded with the sight of his defined jaw, pulsing as he listened intently to her, and his bare chest, broader than the summer before. And those eyes that seemed to penetrate her soul. Not to mention, his scent. And that was just the surface. He was still the most compassionate, creative, and confident person she had ever met. She felt at ease with him. Well, she *had* until now.

There was no mistaking his intention. And *she* knew that he knew that she knew. So even though they didn't actually kiss, there was still no going back. And for that, she was angry at Jeremiah. But the other part of her was angry at herself. Because if she was being truly honest, she hadn't wanted to push him away.

Once they emerged into the light and returned to the picnic spot, Jeremiah helped her to her feet then fetched a towel from the picnic basket.

"What about you?" she asked.

"Looks like I only packed one." He began to rummage through the basket but leapt back with a start. "What the—"

A possum burst out of the basket. A piece of cold pizza hanging haphazardly from its mouth. Its beady eyes darted from Jeremiah then to the foliage nearby where it made its escape.

Jeremiah opened his mouth to speak but only a breathy chuckle came out. The sight of the possum instantly shattered the tension and Crystina doubled over in laughter. Jeremiah's chuckle grew louder until they were both in tears, laughing.

He was breathless. "Since when do possum's eat pizza?"

"You mean, fruit salad." She nodded toward the foliage, a grin igniting her face. "Didn't you see the pineapple?"

"Of course, it would take mine."

"Well, help yourself to my pepperoni. I don't know about you, but I'm not going near that pizza now."

He flashed his lopsided grin and Crystina melted inside.

"Yeah, well, this didn't go to plan, hey?" He shrugged.

"Let's have some tea," she said. "I'm pretty sure possums can't open flasks."

"I don't know... that one was a ninja."

Crystina giggled as she took the thermos and poured its contents into two camper-style mugs and sat down. "Cheers?"

"What are we celebrating?" He joined her on the sandy bank but kept his gaze to the water before them.

"How about Papi?"

Jeremiah's face softened, and he turned to her and picked up one of the mugs of tea. And in that moment, she knew that he knew what that meant. Despite the excitement of Azure Blaze and them reconnecting and all that had happened the last week, there was still a hole in her heart where a wise old man used to be and that would take time to heal.

"I'm sorry about before," Jeremiah said. "I don't know what I was thinking. I won't try anything like that again."

Crystina took a sharp breath and held it. It was the only thing keeping her grounded. That and the mug of hot tea cradled in her palms. She wanted to tell him to try again, to keep testing the waters until she was ready, to convince herself that this was a good idea. But the only words that bubbled to the surface of her confusion were the same two Xavier had offered her so simply. "Thank you."

"To best friends," Jeremiah said. "And to Papi."

"Cheers," she whispered, tapping his mug with her own.

Then she sipped her tea and for the second time that day, everything changed.

Crystina returned home just in time to light the beacon. Chizzy's ears rose to two triangular points as he slept at Abuela's feet. She had fallen asleep in the armchair again, her Bible opened on her lap. Not wanting to disturb her, Crystina took a light blanket and laid it over her then gently kissed her gray hair. She then scratched Chizzy's forehead to tell him he was indeed a good boy.

Once the beacon came to life, rotating as it cast its light across Juniper Bay, Crystina returned to her bedroom to hear a strange vibrating sound. Again and again, it went off until she followed the hum to its source. The burner phone. There were several missed calls, voicemails and text messages. She called Kendra instantly.

"*Azure Blaze, are you alright?*"

"Yeah, sorry, I've been out all day."

She sighed hard. "*Well, praise God for that.*"

"Why? I'm fine."

"*How soon can you meet me at my office?*" she asked.

"Um, straight away, I suppose."

"*Good.*" She paused. "*But... please be careful...*"

Crystina changed into her armored jeans and signature jacket before riding to Juniper City Police

Department. As she entered the front doors, she began to remove her helmet when a familiar voice startled her.

"Not here," Kendra said.

She glanced around from behind the visor. There was an officer on reception but there didn't appear to be anyone else. Then she saw the security cameras overhead. Kendra took her by the elbow and led her to the office. Once the door was safely closed, she nodded her permission, and Crystina slipped her helmet off.

"Okay, what is going on?" she asked. "What was all that?"

Kendra pressed the tips of her fingers to her forehead. "Have a seat."

Hanging her jacket over one of the chairs, Crystina sat down. "You're starting to scare me."

"Tell me, what do you know about St Peter's cathedral in old Juniper town?"

Crystina knew her confusion was visible. She couldn't help it. Her brow scrunched as she remembered the Watchman. "I know it has a new priest. He officiated Papi's funeral service. People call him the Watchman. I don't know why."

"Well, it's ambiguous but I'm not sure if I'd call it suspicious." Kendra leaned back in her chair, her forehead crease deepening. "Azure Blaze, we have discovered a connection between the victims of the recent attacks. *All* the women have been congregants of *that* church specifically."

"*What?*"

"You don't attend, do you?"

"No." She shook her head for emphasis. "No, but he did invite us..."

"I want you to inform me the moment he contacts you or your family. He doesn't know you as Azure Blaze, does he?"

Crystina thought back to her confession. She was certain she hadn't said anything. Then again, there was the incident where she and Chizzy ran three blocks in mere moments. But to avoid concern, she shook her head.

"Well, that's something." Then she looked Crystina square in the eye. "You have to be careful out there. And despite what you say, I'm signing you up for self-defense training. You start Monday."

"What about my job?"

"You start Monday night, then."

Crystina sighed. "Well, that's going to make it a big day."

"Let's just deal with one crisis at a time," Kendra said with a wink.

It sounded good in theory, only Crystina knew it was unlikely to ever deal with one crisis at a time. No, usually when you were down, the Enemy would heap more onto you, and kick you while you were there. If Crystina was a one crisis at a time sort of girl, then she'd be quietly grieving in the safety of the lighthouse, not galivanting to a police station in the middle of the night to assist with a case so closely aligned with the happenings in her life. No, her world had cracked wide open that night the Holy Spirit guided her to old Juniper town. And even though it would have been tempting to ignore that familiar inner voice, to ride aimlessly around the city consumed by all this world had inflicted on her, *listening* was far more life-giving. Perhaps that was why she was still alive, why she survived.

Returning to the lighthouse that night, she was consumed with questions. The loudest though remained that seemingly harmless three letter word. *Why?* Why her? Why not someone else? Was this why her family were safely in heaven, basking in the glory of God, while she was still here? Was this why she survived all those years ago?

She shouldn't have. All the odds had been stacked against her. The cold alone should have put her body into hypothermic shock. Not to mention she had been only six years old and not a strong swimmer. Her elder brothers had been better swimmers. They had spent almost every summer afternoon in the bay, while she tentatively watched from the sand.

Jacob.

Anthony.

Matthew.

Sometimes she wasn't sure if she remembered them or if she just saw their photos so often on the mantel that she just thought she remembered them. She wished she remembered her parents more than she did. But there were only flashes.

Smiles.

Hugs.

Laughter.

She remembered the feeling of them rather than the specifics. Crystina only knew she had her mama's brown eyes from the photographs, but in her heart, she remembered the love in those eyes. She remembered feeling safe as they watched her from across the lawn. She remembered them squinting against the sun as Mama pointed to great blue expanse above. *"Crystina, look, there's a castle made of clouds!"*

Now Mama had her own mansion in the sky.

Crystina shouldn't have been the one to survive.

But here she was...

Why?

CHAPTER 12

Sabbath

Crystina squinted against the first light streaming through her bedroom window. She flicked her desk lamp off and watched the golden light ignite God's Word before her. Her gaze was drawn to Psalm 37, verses five and six: "*Commit your way to the LORD; trust in Him and He will do this: He will make your righteous reward shine like the dawn, your vindication like the noonday sun...*"

Questions had plagued her mind, keeping her from sleep. She was restless. Anxious. But now in the glorious new dawn she could finally see clearly. She didn't have to have all the answers. She just needed to trust the One who did.

A little over a week ago, Papi left this world. Then, the Spirit of God moved through her heart, guiding her steps. At that time, she and Jeremiah had been at the point of becoming estranged until her experience of God brought them back together. Perhaps, a little *too* closely.

Her cheeks warmed at the thought of seeing him today. She hoped he was leading worship. She hadn't heard him sing in what seemed like forever.

She would find out soon enough. For now, she could hear rustling downstairs. Abuela and Chizzy must have been awake. In hindsight, Abuela probably should have named their canine family member. After only one night in Crystina's room, he'd taken to following Abuela's every step. She often almost stood on him, his paws being so big for his body. But he was growing and filling out, and Abuela seemed to enjoy having another mouth to feed, if not the company.

The yellow walls of the kitchen were brightest in the morning, when the sun beamed in through the kitchen window. Abuela had the windows open, making the most of the fresh air before summer's heat took hold of the day. It was the only time of the day Abuela used the oven during a heatwave. The kitchen smelled of freshly baked bread for their communion.

When they arrived at Little Glory Gospel Church later that morning, Ramah, Jeremiah's mom, pulled Crystina into a maternal hug before enveloping Abuela in an embrace of a different kind. Ramah gently held Abuela's hair before she began to stroke it. Then she whispered, from one widow to another, "I am so sorry for your loss."

Abuela's body failed her, and she slumped into Ramah's arms. Ramah rocked her as she had done her five babes when they'd been hurt over years of living wild and free. She had said Isaac, her youngest, practically walked out of her and didn't look back. He was independent. Strong. The perfect bookend to his eldest brother, who Crystina knew to be just the same. Between these two young men, were three equally fierce sisters—Deborah, Viva, and Milcah, or 'Milkie'. One by one, the young women hugged Crystina before Isaac gave her a high-five then ran to the platform at the front.

Jeremiah fell into line. "My turn."

His arms wrapped around her so tight, she could feel his heart thumping against her chest.

Crystina might have been disappointed to learn that Jeremiah wasn't joining the robed choir, was it not for him claiming the seat beside her. His arm brushed hers as he moved to the beat, and his soulful voice, as smooth as melted chocolate, rose to sing *"Hosanna"*.

Big voices brought the small church to life, from a harmonious hum to an epic anthem of praise. Tears pricked Crystina's eyes as the melodious prayer washed over her and lifted her heart, her mind, and her gaze heavenward. Around her, hands and voices rose. Then a mere breath of wind, barely recognizable, skimmed her face. She glanced around.

Take his hand.

She swallowed hard. *What? Why?*

Take hold of his hand.

Lord, what if he gets the wrong idea?

As soon as Crystina silently questioned the Lord, a hint of a smile curled her lips. Would it even *be* the wrong idea?

Surrounded by worshippers, Crystina boldly took hold of Jeremiah's hand. He squeezed hers tight. His was sweaty. Trembling. She tugged on him, drawing his eyes to meet hers.

"What's wrong?" she asked.

He shrugged. "I'm just a little nervous."

Her brow furrowed but as the choir concluded with an angelic "Hallelujah", the congregation sat down, and Crystina followed, biting back more unanswered questions.

"Now," the worship leader began, "we're going to have a word from our brother, Jeremiah."

Crystina's eyes widened.

Jeremiah dropped her hand, picked up his Bible, and rose to the pulpit.

A stirring in Crystina's spirit forced her into silent prayer. *Jesus. Please calm his nerves. Please speak through him. Help him, Lord. Thank You, Jesus.*

She kept her eyes closed as the boy she had known and loved for always and forever cracked the spine of his Bible and commanded the attention of the congregants with the declaration of the Word of God over them. Shivers burst down her arms as the words became living and active in her soul, sharper than any two-edged sword, piercing her heart. She hung on God's every word, spoken through this boy who was becoming a man before her very eyes.

With her spiritual nerve endings exposed, Crystina received a word for him that could only have come from Jesus. Because she knew it was the furthest thing from Jeremiah's plans.

This is his path.

Crystina's eyes flew open just in time to catch Jeremiah staring in her direction with the Word of God on his lips, his voice fueled by the power of the Holy Spirit. Her mouth was suddenly dry. *This* was his path? What about JCU? What about the career he desired, the financial security to take care of his family?

This is his path.

Crystina blinked up at the bright lights above the pulpit. *But, Lord, You know his dad was a preacher, and You know he left the family with hardship and debt when he died. There's no way...*

THIS IS HIS PATH.

She shrunk back in her seat a little, feeling the conviction of the Holy Spirit burning within her, nullifying any excuses she brought to the table.

Well, if this was Jeremiah's path, then he wasn't going to like it.

Crystina didn't know how to broach the subject with Jeremiah, so she made an excuse to leave early—an easy feat when living with an elderly woman—and slipped away with Abuela for a simple Sunday lunch. Usually Sundays meant a high-end roast and maybe even a nap to aid the digestion. But not today. Today, the only man in the house bounded around on four paws and would have happily eaten straight from the can if she'd let him.

Abuela took her sandwich to her bedroom, claiming tiredness.

Crystina took her sandwich to the lantern room and watched the clouds shift as she ate, trying to see if she could spot a fluffy white castle. As she sat there, searching, her phone buzzed.

"Can we talk?"

Usually, her response to this question coming from Jeremiah would be instant. But she hesitated.

Then he added. *"Please?"*

"Sure thing." She typed and regretted it instantly. What would she say? Would God force her to speak up? What if she wasn't ready?

"Beach, okay?"

"See you in a bit."

Her steps were heavy, hesitant as she changed out of her Sunday dress into shorts and one of her dad's old band t-shirts. It was so faded but once upon a time it had smelled like him, and she liked to imagine it still did.

Jeremiah was waiting on the line of sand bordering the tide, just damp enough to leave an impression but far enough away so the waves only touched his toes. He didn't even see her approach. His gaze was fixated on the horizon, his back weighed down as he leaned forward, elbows resting on his knees.

"Hey," she said softly, "you okay?"

He didn't meet her eye. He didn't even move. Then his eyes narrowed slightly before he asked, "Why did you hold my hand in church?"

Crystina bit her lip and sat down beside him. He probably thought she was playing games, leading him on. She wasn't. She just needed time. And answers.

"You don't understand," he went on, "I really need to know."

"He told me to," she said softly.

Jeremiah slowly nodded.

Crystina shifted uneasily on the damp sand as it clung to her bare legs. "Jerry? Aren't you going to talk to me?"

He exhaled heavily. "I didn't think you'd do it."

"What are you talking about?"

"I asked Him for a sign," he said. "I said if you took hold of my hand in front of the congregation that I'd know what He'd been telling me was right... But I didn't think you'd do it..."

Crystina wanted to hold his hand even now but so much was stopping her. Their friendship could be ruined. But most of all, she knew what happened to people who came too close to her. One way or another, they got hurt.

"He's calling you to be a preacher," she said.

His jaw pulsed. "I can't do it, Crys. I just can't."

She stared at his hand. How she wanted to hold it again and tell him it would all be okay. But the lines had been blurred already and if she was going to protect him, then she needed to keep her distance.

She placed a hand on his back, the way any regular friend might, and she felt him relax beneath her touch. "How long have you been avoiding it?"

"I felt it all senior year. I could've said no to the scholarship. But I didn't."

"So, what are you going to do?"

"Didn't you hear what I said? I can't do it!" He stood up. "I've seen that life. I've seen my mom struggle to put food on the table. I want better for her. I want better for y—" He stopped himself. "For *me*. I want better than that."

She climbed to her feet. "What about if what He has *is* better?"

"I won't be a college drop-out," he said. "Not after I worked so hard to get in."

"Your mom would understand..."

"Of course, she would. She followed my dad's every whim!" He began to pace the sand. "We almost had to live on the street, Crystina. If it wasn't for the church stepping in. My dad almost ruined all of our lives!"

She shook her head. "Jeremiah, your dad was a good man. More importantly, he was a godly man. And he followed Jesus Christ right to the end of his days, so don't you dare speak ill of him." Crystina choked back a sob. "Don't you dare!"

His face softened. And that was when Crystina fully noticed his graying complexion, his dark circles.

"Jerry," she said softly. "What's really going on?"

"I'm struggling is all. I'm struggling to keep up. To hand assignments in on time. To attend classes with my part time job at the church."

"You're working at the church? Why didn't you tell me?"

"Because I didn't want you to make a big deal of it," he snapped. "I don't want to be a preacher. I'm doing a church history elective. That should be enough! And at the church, I just help out and fill in and I don't want to—"

"It's not about you!" Crystina bit back, her frustration at boiling point. "Do you think I want to do this whole Azure Blaze thing?"

He folded his hands behind his head and turned away. "Oh, here we go..."

"What?"

"Don't pull some holier than thou—"

"Excuse me?!"

He fixed his gaze on the horizon again.

"I don't know who you are right now," Crystina choked. "But my best friend would never speak to me like that..."

"Well, maybe your best *friend*—"

"*Don't.*"

His bloodshot eyes shifted to her.

"Don't even go there, Jeremiah," she said, and began to retrace her steps. "Stay away from me."

CHAPTER 13

Defender

On Monday evening, the officers of Juniper City Police Department wouldn't know what hit them. Crystina marched in as Azure Blaze, head high, flaming jacket tossed over her shoulder, boots thumping. A new fire burned beneath her skin. A righteous anger. Holy indignation. After a morning spent praying through her confusion over Jeremiah and St Peters and all the unanswered questions, she burst into Kendra's office with a chip on her shoulder and pent-up frustration to unleash.

She whipped off her helmet. "I'm ready."

Kendra blinked up at her. "Are you alright?"

"Let's just do this."

Without a word, Kendra rounded the desk and led the way back out down the hall to a coded door. More corridors led to a large shed-like arena with boxing mannequins placed between ropes courses. In the center of the arena stood a boxing ring. To her far right were a set of windows behind which a male officer stood, pistol in hand, aiming and firing at the targets that swam past his vision.

"The glass is bullet proof," Kendra said, "so you can relax."

"I wasn't nervous," she replied. And it was true. She had committed this day to God. She had sat at the dining table with Abuela, taken the sacraments, and claimed the blood of Christ over their family. She wasn't nervous. If she looked tense, it was because she was angry.

"So, what's first?" Her eyes scanned the arena, her restlessness flaring.

"Beep test."

"Huh?"

"We need to assess your fitness level." Kendra strode over to a boombox set on a stool.

Red lines on the floor marked Crystina's start and finish positions. She inwardly groaned and stripped off her armored motorcycle jeans to reveal her active wear beneath then pulled her hair into a ponytail. Crystina was never one for track, but she obediently crouched at the first red line.

"And.... go!"

She lunged into a sprint.

"Pace yourself," Kendra warned.

But Crystina wouldn't listen. She was here to prove a point. If not for herself, then for Jeremiah. Crystina was grateful she hadn't confided in him about working with the JCPD. Now she knew there had to be boundaries with Jeremiah. He had kept his God-given calling a secret from her for one reason and one reason only—he didn't want to fulfill it. He wanted to be the college guy. The successful guy. The one who went on to do things the rest of them wished they could. When it got to their senior school reunion, he didn't want to be the one admitting he was a small-town preacher. He had watched his dad take that narrow path and he didn't want to follow those footprints. How strange then, that Jeremiah preached at all. It was as if he was trying to satisfy God and himself at the same time.

Frustrated and confused, Crystina finally collapsed on the floor in a heap. All the beep test had proved was that she was below average in the fitness department and prone to distraction.

Kendra shook her head. "Don't get too comfortable down there. When you're ready, give me fifty."

"Um, fifty *what?*"

"Push-ups."

Crystina hadn't done pushups since gym class, and even then she would claim it was 'that time of the month' to sit them out. Still, if she was going to practice self-defense, then she wanted to do it right.

"I don't see how this is helping," she groaned as she pushed her body up for the tenth time.

Kendra smirked. "Eleven—and you wouldn't—twelve!"

"Can't we... make it... *twenty?*"

"Fine. Only this once," Kendra said. "But next time, I won't be so soft. Fifteen!"

"Next time?" She pushed harder and the tension began to course from her mind to her arms to the floor. A shifting of energy. "This isn't a one time thing?"

Kendra chuckled. "Eighteen."

As Crystina forced her way through the next pushup, her arms burned. Her heart thumped against her chest. Clarity pierced her mind and confusion began to dissolve. If Jeremiah wasn't going to follow God's call on his life, then that was his problem, and God would have to call him on that. She couldn't fix him. Crystina had to focus on her own calling and if that meant her path no longer entwined with Jeremiah's then that was just the way it had to be. Though she did wonder where her and Abuela would attend church on Sunday. Could they go to St Peters? Could she risk it? What if something happened to Abuela? And why was someone targeting a church of all places? She knew the wider culprit—the Enemy—of course, he would attack a church and its people. But who was he using to do his bidding? And why were they so set on derailing this particular house of worship?

"Azure Blaze!" Kendra shouted.

Panting, Crystina rolled onto her back and looked up at her, confused.

"You really didn't hear me?" She held out her hand. "That was thirty."

Crystina took her hand and yanked on it, letting her take her full weight, much like she did with Jeremiah. Or used to. Yesterday would take more than an apology to make things right. He needed to change his path and she wasn't sure if he was prepared to do that. If he wouldn't do it for God or even for himself, then he certainly wouldn't do it for her.

"So where does that mind of yours keep running to?" Kendra asked.

She shook her head, relishing in the clarity her burning body was bringing to her mind. "Next. What's next?"

Kendra nodded toward the center of the arena. "Ring. Let's teach you a few things."

"Will I be training with you?"

"Don't worry, we'll start slow," Kendra said, the same deep strength in her voice. "I'm here to *train* you, not to whip your butt."

Kendra made it look effortless sliding in between the ropes. Crystina fumbled in, ending up prematurely on her bottom.

"We can work on your balance later." Kendra helped her to her feet again. "Now, one thing you need to remember is how to execute an effective palm strike. This one move has gotten me out of a lot of trouble." She met Crystina's eye. "A *lot* of trouble, you hear?"

She nodded.

"Good. Now, push my shoulder with the palm of your hand. No fingers. Just your palm."

"Okay." Crystina shook her hands loose then flung her right hand forward, her palm thumping into Kendra's shoulder.

"Good. But harder."

Crystina tried again.

"Good. This is getting you used to using your palm. Again. I just felt your fingers, Azure Blaze. Palm only!"

Crystina formed a firm hand, palm forward and shoved her again.

"Nice. Harder."

"I don't want to hurt you," she said between pushes.

Kendra took hold of her hand and twisted Crystina's arm until she held her in a headlock. "Azure Blaze, you do not worry about hurting me right now. If our God calls you to a situation where you need to defend yourself, even in the most basic way, then I need to know that you can do it, okay?" She released her. "Now, girl. Harder!"

Fueled and ready, Crystina pushed her palm as hard as she could into Kendra's shoulder once more, forcing Kendra to stumble back ever so slightly.

"That's what I'm talking about! Now, *quicker.*"

Crystina increased her pace, striking her shoulder.

"Good. Now that's hitting me with your palm. Nice!"

Crystina stepped back to take a breath.

"Remember, if you're using a palm strike at the chin—" Kendra stretched her head back. "Then it naturally arches the body, leaving it open particularly for a kick to the groin." Kendra clapped her hands and swiped a boxing mitt from the sides. "Okay, now let's see a kick..."

Crystina remembered Jeremiah's words yesterday, warning her not to be 'holier than thou'. Her skin crawled with frustration, and she channeled it into every kick, every knee of the mitt. Kendra urged her on. Harder. Quicker. Higher. Then the wind of the fan skimmed her sweaty face. Crystina flicked her hair. Her body pivoted. Her feet switched positions and before she could pause to recognize her own limitations, Crystina's foot flew in a back kick, sending the mitt flying across the arena.

Kendra stared at her. "Okay, *who* taught you that?"

Crystina's fists were raised in defense before her chest. "No one. I just... did it."

The wonder in Kendra's eyes was unmistakable. Crystina knew that look. It was the same one she saw in the mirror when God did something unexplainable.

"Well, let's take this to the dummys," Kendra said with a grin.

When Crystina was unleashed on the freestanding boxing bags, she was surprised by her own agility. She wielded her palm strike with ease and followed it up with a knee to the groin or a spinning back kick to the abdomen. Unlike the sprinting, there was an ease that came to moving her body in this way. There was structure. There was the application of knowledge. But beyond that, there was the Spirit of God bracing her elbow, thrusting her palm forward, stabilizing her balance when she thought she would waver. He was there with her. Aiding her efforts. Strengthening her because she showed up and followed the call. For the first time in a long time, her mind was clear. Her shoulders loosened. Tension dissolved as she began to think of this time as worship. She fully dedicated every movement to honoring God, to giving glory to Him, because He was the one making this possible right now. Not her. Any agility she brought to this arena was purely by the grace of God raining over her life. She remembered David going into the valley with his slingshot and a few mere stones. Here was her giant. *This* challenge. This new narrow path of Azure Blaze. And all Crystina had was a slingshot and river stones. She didn't have the experience to wield a sword or to expertly move in armor other than that required for her motorbike. No, she only came with a willingness to follow the will of God the Father. But as it happened, that was all she needed. For as she pivoted into one final back kick, the dummy lost its balance and flew to the floor with an almighty thump. Her Goliath was slain.

When Crystina returned to the lighthouse at twilight, just in time to light the beacon, Jeremiah was waiting on the front lawn.

Crystina pulled off her helmet. "I don't have time right now."

"Crys, wait..." He reached for her but retracted his hand with a single look from her.

"Not now," she said, pushing past him. "I told you to stay away from me, and I meant it."

And for the first time in her life, she closed the door on Jeremiah Sanderson.

With legs of jelly, she ascended the spiral staircase, each step heavier than the one before. She lit the beacon then collapsed on the cool floor and gazed out at the changing sky. Her throat was hoarse from the exercise. She sniffed back the tears threatening to form like storm clouds and desperately tried to hold onto the clarity and calm she had found in that arena.

She was just tired. That's all those tears were. Exhaustion.

She'd almost lost Jeremiah before, when their friendship had dwindled to the occasional text and waving from across the bay. She could lose him again and survive just fine.

CHAPTER 14

The Gates of St Peter's

The morning after her first day of self-defense training, Crystina hobbled into Legion International Media, past the rows of junior assistants to her exclusive workstation. It was barely 8am, but an extra-large takeaway coffee sat on Crystina's pristine desk with a broad smiley face on the lid beneath the letter 'S' scrawled in black.

"I thought you might need it," Xavier said from the doorway to his office.

"Thanks. But I think you have our roles slightly reversed."

"Tell you what," he leaned against the doorframe, "I'll let you get them tomorrow."

Crystina braced herself on the arms of her swivel chair and eased herself into it. Her whole body burned. Her limbs ached. Even reaching for her coffee seemed too heavy a task.

"What's wrong with *you*?"

"I... er... joined a gym." She forced a smile. Yesterday she had felt like dynamite. Today she felt like the burnt-out wick after the explosion.

"Right. Well, I'd like another exclusive on Azure Blaze this week," Xavier said. "Could you let Emma know?"

"Absolutely."

He nodded once. "Well, as you were then."

She watched him disappear again before she slouched back into the chair and stared dimly at her set of headphones. It would require lifting her arms to put them on her head and she wasn't sure if she was ready for that level of commitment. She glanced at the coffee which was at arm level. Now that seemed more achievable. Besides, it wasn't even technically her start time yet. As she took a sip, she heard her own phone vibrate. Another message from Jeremiah. She'd lost count of how many he'd sent or how many voicemails he'd left. Not only was he ignoring what the Lord was clearly calling him to do, he hadn't even told her about it, and then lashed out when she had called him out on it. Of course, then, there was the intrusive thought that if he hadn't accepted the scholarship then it would have gone to another student and that other student could have been her. She shook her head. It was a waste of time thinking about such things now. That season of her life was over. This was her life now. Whatever *this* was. She still wasn't entirely sure, especially since she had accepted the role of personal assistant.

Once she had mustered the strength and concentration to put the headphones on, she dialed Emma's extension.

Her sweet voice filtered through the headphones. "Good morning, this is Emma!"

"Hey Em," she said into the mic, "it's Crystina. How are you?"

She squealed down the line. "Oh my goodness! I'm fantastic, how are you? Did you read my article? How cool is Azure Blaze?"

Crystina smiled to herself. "Pretty cool... I can't believe you got to talk to her in person."

"I know. Me too."

"So how's the new job?"

"I'm still pinching myself," Emma said wistfully. "Somehow I've ended up where I always wanted to be."

"And it's good?"

"Ye-ah... most of the time. It's still hard, you know. Being a reporter is way harder than dreaming about being one." She snorted.

"Speaking of which, Xavier would like another exclusive on Azure Blaze. Do you think you could get one?"

"Hmm, I don't know. I mean, she contacted me last time..."

"But she has only spoken to you," Crystina said. "Surely that carries some weight?"

"Yeah, I mean, I guess I could ask around at church?"

Crystina tried to act surprised. "Oh, you go to church? Which one?"

"St Peters in old Juniper town. Do you know it?"

Crystina's stomach plummeted within her. "Yeah," she mustered, "I do. It's, um, a really beautiful building but I've never been to a service as such."

"You totally should."

"Hey, I have to see Xavier about something but let me know if you need a hand with your article, okay?"

"Will do! And maybe we can hang out sometime? Like, outside of work?"

Crystina smiled to herself. "I'd really like that. Speak to you soon."

After she disconnected, she rose from her seat so quickly she almost forgot her pain. But her body swiftly reminded her, forcing her to hunch over.

She peered into Xavier's office. "Hey, would you like a bagel with that coffee?"

Xavier scoffed. "What, and ruin all your hard work at the gym?"

"There's this place in old Juniper town that makes the best blueberry bagels. Wholewheat, of course," she said then added, "Unless you have some dry cleaning for me to collect or something?"

He sighed. "Go on then. Bagels it is."

When Crystina arrived at St Peter's—with the mental note to collect bagels on her way back to the office—the Watchman already sat in the front pew as though waiting for something. Or someone. He gazed pensively at the altar before him. Silent.

Crystina cleared her throat.

"It is quite all right," the Watchman said over his shoulder, "you are very welcome here."

She smiled as she approached. "Thank you. I just have a few questions."

"You are not here for confession?" He shifted his weight to his walking aid as he rose.

"Not today." Crystina let out a breathy laugh. "I actually have a few questions about the women of your congregation who have been targeted recently."

"Of course," the Watchman said. "I have a few questions about that myself."

Crystina's brow arched. "Oh?"

"However, I will share with you what I *do* know."

Crystina sat beside him, listening expectantly.

"I have only been here a short while," the Watchman said. "Prior to my arrival, St Peter's was on the verge of selling its land. Congregants and, therefore, tithes were on the decline. There was a buyer lined up for the purchase. However, the church received a miraculous donation. A sizeable sum. Enough to sustain the church in its time of need—that was when the threats started. The attacks. The previous priest did not know what to make of it, so he walked away."

"He just up and left?" Crystina asked.

"Yes, and I was commanded to step in," the Watchman said.

"Sounds like you're employed by some sort of taskmaster." She laughed nervously. "So, who was the buyer?"

"There were little details on the matter, just an agreed sum," the Watchman said and pulled out a pocket-sized notebook from his robe. "However, I did happen to come across the city address where the buyer is said to have been located." He skimmed through the pages, occasionally licking his finger to assist, then he handed the small double-spread to Crystina.

Crystina peered down. The address was written in thick black marker, probably for the Watchman's poor eyesight, but it meant that there was no mistaking it.

"Are you sure this is right?" she asked.

"Most certainly."

She studied the address again before she confirmed aloud. "That's Legion International Media…"

CHAPTER 15

Zero Interest?

"For your ways are in full view of the LORD,
and He examines all your paths."

PROVERBS 5:21

What am I doing here? Jeremiah took a long gulp of his cappuccino and winced. It was too hot to drink fast.

Harper sipped her latte. "Well, this is nice."

"Mmm." He glanced around and hoped his presence would go unnoticed. Out of all the places in Juniper City, Harper had to suggest *this* one. It was on the same block as Legion International Media, which meant, yes, close to her work, but also dangerously close to Crystina's work. And *that* confrontation was the last thing he needed after their fight the other day.

The coffee shop buzzed, new orders were balanced by the tray load out the door, and customers continually raced in with new ones. In all this hustle, surely no one would recognize him.

"So why did you want to see me?" Jeremiah asked.

"A question for a question." She shrugged. "Why did you suddenly agree? I thought you said you weren't interested."

"I'm not." He bit his lip. He was going to have to be careful if he wanted her help. "I mean, not in *that* way."

She leaned back in her chair. "That's okay, I can be pretty persuasive."

"You don't get it." He skidded his chair back slightly. He was ready to up and walk if she tried anything. It wasn't that Harper wasn't attractive in the typical sense. She always dressed to impress and made sure she was never caught with a single blonde hair out of place. Most guys would go crazy over a girl like Harper. But Jeremiah wasn't most guys. At least, not anymore.

"Wait, don't go—" She reached for his hand, but he raised them as though she was armed.

"The only reason I came here was to pick your brain about Crystina," he said.

Her make-up cracked slightly when she furrowed her brow. "Seriously?"

"I'm out of ideas. She doesn't see me as anything other than a friend."

"Wow, okay. I guess some things never change."

He drank some more coffee before meeting her eye.

As stubborn and tenacious as Harper tended to be, there was a slight satisfaction igniting those intense blue eyes. Amusement flickered across her face, and she folded her arms across her chest. "Well, I have twenty minutes before I have to start work, so you better talk fast."

"Really?"

"Jerry." She sighed. "The sooner you and Crystina acknowledge your feelings for each other, the better for everyone involved."

He leaned in. "Yeah, but I tried to kiss her, and she just pulled away."

"In what situation?"

"We were swimming." He shrugged.

"Jeremiah Sanderson, what is wrong with you? Seriously, I want to know. Even I know she's terrified of water—"

"But—"

"I'm not finished." She narrowed her eyes. "How could you do that to her? She would have been feeling so vulnerable, and after the week from hell she's had losing her grandfather, and then you sweep in and try to take advantage of her?"

"That's not how it was."

"Well, that's how it sounds." Her voice turned stern. "You can't exploit her grief, Jerry. You have to be more sensitive. You know what she's like. Everything she has been through..."

Jeremiah might have smirked were it not for the truth in her words. Who knew, Harper Lloyd could render him speechless?

"What else have you done?" She gulped her latte.

"We may have had a fight the other night as well..."

"May have or *did*?"

"Did."

"About?"

"The particulars don't really matter," he said.

"They do if you want my help."

"Well..." He didn't even really know where to begin. "It snowballed pretty quickly. One minute we were talking about my calling—work, study, stuff like that—and the next, well... she told me to stay away from her."

Harper's eyebrows arched. "Okay, well that sounds very unlike her. What made her say that?"

He was ashamed even to say it out loud. It was a moment of weakness. He hadn't meant it. It had come from that dark place he had been trying so hard to suppress. It was the same dark place that niggled at him and spurred him on to do things he wouldn't normally do. Like, accept a coffee invitation from Harper Lloyd.

143

It's just coffee, he had told himself. *Well, yeah, of course she's hot but I'm not interested... I want to be with Crystina... but she did tell me to stay away from her, so...*

You could just settle, the dark place had said. *Then you wouldn't have to "wait" for more...*

That was when he shook his head and rebuked the thought, claiming 2 Corinthians chapter ten verse five that told him to take every thought captive to make it obedient to Christ.

"I told her not to do the whole holier than thou thing with me," he admitted.

She nodded slowly. "And?"

"Just acted like a jerk in general, I guess."

"Because you're frustrated?"

"No," he said impulsively, then replaced his answer, "well, yeah, I guess, but not in the way you're suggesting."

"Jerry, this is me." Harper drained her glass then stared him down. "Have you told her about us?"

His hunger for more caffeine swiftly wasted away and he stared at his cup. "It was one time."

"Yeah, well, it was a fairly significant one time." She shrugged. "But whatever, at the end of the day it's your business, but you might want to try a bit of honesty. It can go a long way."

"She'll never want me if she finds out."

Harper slipped out from her seat. "Well, I have to go but Crystina deserves to know that if you *do* end up together that she wouldn't be your first."

Jeremiah's face burned. It was true, he wasn't most guys... *anymore*. Once upon a time, he had been. Back when he assumed Crystina was out of reach and Harper had run away from home again after her dad had been on the booze again. After that night, the next thing he knew she was inviting him to the dance, and he had to admit his true feelings. It was just one time. One moment of weakness. He had felt sorry for her. He had only wanted to comfort her, but one thing had led to another and—

"Crystina!" Harper gasped. "How long have you been standing—"

The double take-away coffee order tumbled from Crystina's hands as she stared at Jeremiah.

He felt himself shrink and panic drained his face. "Crystina... I can explain..."

She beelined for the front door, briefly waving to the waitress and calling an apology over her shoulder before escaping onto the street.

Jeremiah bolted after her. "Crystina!"

"I told you to stay away from me." She conquered the short sidewalk route to the office in moments.

He grabbed her hand.

She yanked it away.

"Please," he said, "let me explain!"

"I have *zero interest* in anything you have to say!"

He jolted as his own words left her mouth. And so, his determined pursuit came to a blunt stop and Crystina disappeared through the rotating doors of Legion International Media.

CHAPTER 16

Battleground

"Where's my coffee?" Xavier's voice traveled through her headphones.

"Oh, I, um." She shook her head and glanced up through the glass wall separating them. "I'm sorry, I'll get some more."

"More? What, you drank them both?"

She grabbed her bag. "It's not that."

"Hey—"

It was not her morning. First, she slept in and had to rush out the door without so much as a single Bible verse to take into the day. Then her mind and heart had been blown wide open in the coffee shop down the street and now her body was protesting to the smallest movements. Crystina tried to escape but Xavier caught up to her without effort. It seemed the adrenaline from the coffee shop had waned. In those moments on the street, she had been completely numb to her post-training body. Now, she was acutely aware of the second day rule of exercise—it always hurt more than the first.

"Hey!" Xavier took hold of her arm and spun her around to face him.

She stared up at him with stinging eyes. "I'm fine."

"Uh-huh, you don't look fine. Come to my office." He tugged her arm. "I'll order us both a coffee and you can tell me what's going on."

She pulled back. "I can do it. I said I'm—"

"Santos," he said with a low tone. "Don't think I won't throw you over my shoulder."

She stopped struggling. "You wouldn't."

"Try me."

Her frown deepened. The last thing she wanted was a heart to heart with Amos Xavier, especially after what she had just overheard. But neither did she want to deal with the office gossip were he to literally carry her to his office. "Haven't you got anything better to do?"

He didn't answer her question but closed the door and pressed a button beneath his desk that tinted the glass.

"I didn't know you could do that."

"Yes, well, I'm full of surprises." He punched onto his phone with his thumbs. "And no, I don't have anything *better* to do. Coffee is a vital part of the day. Hazelnut latte, right?"

She was about to decline and go for a more 'grown-up' beverage but who was she kidding, it was divine. "Yes please."

"There, done." He placed his phone face down. "Now, what's going on?"

"I think I have to resign," she said.

"Crystina," he began gently, "what's going on?"

"You'll think it's crazy."

"Crazier than hearing God speak to you?"

He had a point.

"Try me," he said.

She exhaled hard. "Well, I just overheard a conversation I shouldn't have. Down in the coffee shop. And now that I *know*, I feel like it changes everything. He has kept so much from me, I can't believe it... He's the first person I want to share things with. But obviously, he doesn't feel the same."

"The boyfriend, right? Joey?"

"He's not my boyfriend. And it's Jerry."

"I thought—"

"I let you think that." She sighed. "Maybe because I wanted him to be? Maybe because I knew about your reputation with girls..."

"I don't know what you're talking about."

She rolled her eyes.

He watched her closely. "Okay, so what has all of this got to do with resigning? And by the way, your contract forbids you to resign."

"No, it doesn't."

"Okay, no, *technically* it doesn't. But it would be incredibly inconvenient if you did resign."

In that moment, there was a knock on the door and Harper carried in a cardboard tray with two takeaway coffees. "Sorry, sir, these were just delivered."

Crystina stiffened.

"That's fine, just place them on the desk."

Crystina kept her eyes on the plaque with Xavier's name, studying the bevel of the edge, the lines on the serif font.

"You went to the same senior school as my lovely assistant, didn't you, Miss Lloyd?" Xavier asked.

Harper cleared her throat. "Yes, yes I did."

Xavier's stare burned into Crystina forcing her to meet it.

"So you must know Jerry," he said before leaning across the table. "Is that right? It was *Jerry* wasn't it?"

There was a weight to his question. Crystina knew he wasn't just confirming his name. He was determining something else entirely.

"Yes," Crystina said at last. "That's right."

"Hmm." He nodded. "Oh, and by the way, Miss Lloyd. You'll be moving to the fifth floor to assist in the accounts department."

Harper's mouth fell open. "What?!"

"Yeah, *what?*" Crystina repeated, just as shocked.

Harper glanced to Crystina then back to Xavier. "I'm terrible with numbers."

"You seem like the type of girl who likes a challenge," he said with a tight smile.

Crystina shifted uncomfortably in the chair.

"I don't understand, sir," Harper began, seemingly ready to continue when Xavier raised his hand.

"That'll be all Miss Lloyd. Fifth floor."

Harper withdrew in silence and the moment the door shuddered closed, Xavier reached for his earpiece.

"What are you doing?" Crystina asked.

"Calling in a favor with the accounts department." He shrugged. "I guess they could always use an assistant, right? I'm doing them a favor really parting with one of my junior assistants... Ah, yes, hi Charles! It's Amos Xavier here... well, funny story actually..."

Crystina took her hazelnut latte and slipped away before Xavier decided to sue the coffee shop for making it too hot and burning her mouth. What was with him? In truth, she probably couldn't financially afford to resign, but neither could she emotionally afford to work with Harper Lloyd after what she just discovered.

"I thought you'd be out soon." Harper was waiting at Crystina's workstation. "Now that you got your way."

"I didn't ask for this."

"Well, I don't know why you're so upset anyway. It's not like you and Jerry are even together."

By God's grace, Crystina bit back all the defenses she wanted to hurl at Harper. She skirted the desk and managed to sit down without wincing.

"And Jerry only wants you anyway," Harper went on. "He always has."

Crystina sipped her hazelnut latte. "Not always, apparently. See you round, Harper. I have work to do."

Placing her coffee cup beside her diary, Crystina picked up her headphones and started dialing. Thankfully, Harper took the hint, and Crystina could hang up before Abuela answered.

"Would you believe it, I had one of those prank calls today." Abuela tutted. "They just hung up before I could even answer..."

Abuela shook her head and continued to potter in the kitchen. Melchizedek had given up following under her feet—no doubt after his own paws had been trodden on—and lay on the mat by the sink, his tail wagging whenever Abuela walked past him.

"It was me," Crystina confessed and curled her legs up beneath herself on the couch.

Abuela untied her apron and rested it on the kitchen bench; a sign that profound wisdom was about to ensue. Small sobs escaped from Crystina, and she felt like a child once more whose world had just been shattered by loss. Only this time, she was grieving a dream she didn't even know was truly there until it had been taken away.

She had wanted to be Jeremiah's first.

And she wanted *him*.

There was no use denying it anymore. Her reaction confirmed it, the aching in her soul was a constant reminder of the truth. She hadn't wanted to accept it. But now she had been confronted by the thought of him with someone else.

"Jerry, this is me. Have you told her about us?" Harper's voice went round and round in her head. *Us.* Jeremiah and Harper. They had an *us.*

Crystina's heart had stopped when she heard his name in that coffee shop; when she had turned, tray in hand, to see him with *her.*

"She'll never want me if she finds out..."

How Crystina wished that was true.

"... Crystina deserves to know that if you do end up together that she wouldn't be your first."

Yes, she did deserve to know, but not in the way she found out. There should have been sensitivity and care. Instead, the truth had brutally landed on her while being tossed haphazardly around.

Crystina hadn't understood the difficulty in keeping the Ten Commandments until now, because now she wanted something she would never have. Number ten—do not covet. Well, here she was. Coveting.

Abuela wedged herself onto the end of the couch, and gently pulled Crystina to lay her head on her lap. Abuela smelled of tomato and basil. She stroked Crystina's hair, lulling her into a place of vulnerability. *"This little light of mine,"* Abuela sang gently, *"I'm gonna let it shine..."*

Heavier sobs overtook Crystina as she listened to the only song she remembered her mama singing over her at bedtime. The only song that calmed her spirit when nothing else could. The calling her mama had spoken over her in those fragile years before her family was snatched away from her.

"This little light of mine, I'm gonna let it shine. This little light of mine, I'm gonna let it shine. Let it shine. Let it shine. Let it shine..."

Crystina cleared her thick throat. *"Hide it under a bushel? No..."* She choked back the tears. *"I'm gonna let it shine."*

Abuela continued. *"Hide it under a bushel? No. I'm gonna let it shine. Hide it under a bushel. No. I'm gonna let it shine. Let it shine. Let it shine. Let it shine..."*

"Everywhere I go," Crystina whispered, "I'm gonna let it shine..."

Abuela leaned down and kissed her hair. "So, my little warrior, what's going on with you?"

"I don't know." Hot tears swept down Crystina's cheeks. She couldn't tell Abuela about Jeremiah. Ironically, she felt as though that would be a betrayal. But she could tell her about the repercussions of the past few days. It had all made her feel disconnected from God. "I feel so distracted. I haven't heard the Lord speak again. What if I'm not meant to be Azure Blaze? What if I got it all wrong?"

"Then you were a hero for a week. It's not the worst thing in the world. However, I sense that is not the issue here."

Crystina reared her head. "What do you mean?"

Did Abuela know? Had the Lord revealed something to her? Crystina knew all too well the hours Abuela spent on her knees before the Lord; no doubt grateful for those knee replacements. Her Bible was always at hand. A prayer always on her lips. And now communion had become part of her morning routine as she remembered the victory of the resurrection of Jesus Christ. Abuela was a prayer warrior. A mighty woman of God. The Proverbs 31 woman personified. So, if Crystina in all her weaknesses was still hearing the voice of the Spirit of God in her life, she couldn't even comprehend how Abuela must know Him.

"You are under spiritual attack," she declared with conviction. "The enemy is throwing distractions at you because he knows you have been called to do Kingdom work."

She sniffled then nestled back into Abuela's lap. "Well, this time he's distracting me with Jerry."

"Ah, I see."

"I don't know how I feel about Jeremiah now."

"You don't have to have the answers right now," Abuela hushed her and returned to stroking her hair. "Talk to Jesus about it. See what He has to say."

"Well, I know I will have to forgive him." She smiled weakly and hoped Abuela wouldn't ask any questions. "But I don't even know how to forgive and move forward without getting hurt again."

"I wish I had the answers for you. But whenever I had a disagreement with your papi—may the Lord rest his soul—I would take it to *Him* in prayer." She pointed to the ceiling and beyond. "And to confession, of course. I liked to think the priest gave Papi a little talking to after the next mass."

Crystina smiled.

"Now, there's my little warrior." Abuela smoothed a tear from Crystina's cheek. "I am going to tell you what the priest back in my country used to tell me." She placed her hand on Crystina's hair, as though praying over her. "This is not about you or him." Renewing strength flowed through her words. "The enemy is at work, trying to destroy what you have built because your relationship brings glory to God. So, be strong in the Lord and in His *mighty* power. Put on the *full* armor of God, so that you can take your stand against the enemy's schemes. For our struggle is not against flesh and blood. So put on the armor of God so that when evil comes knocking on your door, you will be equipped to stand your ground. And after you have done everything... to stand."

Crystina rose to sit upright on the couch, defying the heaviness of her tear-congested head and her aching body. How had she allowed the enemy to use Jeremiah to distract her and make her doubt her calling? She had to set things right. First, with God. Then with Jerry.

CHAPTER 17

Wanted

In the shadows of dusk, Melchizedek bounded ahead. Crystina wandered the esplanade, praying in her heart for direction. The beacon briefly ignited her path on its rotation, but it would move on without fail, leaving her in the near darkness.

She listened for the waves, for the stillness of the night, for the wind rushing over the waves toward her. Ocean breezes stirred through her hair, flicking it over her shoulder. She peered back. There across the bay stood the Sanderson home. She knew it was their dinner time and that it would be beautiful chaos. Her heart longed to be there, and in that moment, there was a tugging in her spirit, calling her to that old familiar place she used to know as her home away from home.

Go.

She took a sharp breath. "What?" she gasped aloud. *"Really?"*

Yes. Go.

Crystina imagined Jesus smiling at her, giving her permission to go against logical thought and follow her heart across the bay.

"Chizzy!" She started to run toward the Sanderson home.

He accepted the challenge and bounded in the opposite direction to where he had been heading. He met her pace then overtook quickly, all limbs and paws, his tail frantic. When they reached the front screen door, a delicious, homey scent wafted toward her to complement the golden glow from the inside. The solid door was open to let the fresh sea air into the home. Crystina braced herself, wanting to knock, but fearful. What if Jeremiah didn't want to see her? What was he just saying about his mama having too many mouths to feed? She hesitated. She wanted to say that she had already eaten but after Abuela's inspiring talk, Crystina had lit the beacon and then headed out for a walk and some much needed prayer. She couldn't deny that she was starving. Perhaps she should just return home? Come back another time when it wasn't family dinner and when she was expected...

"Crystina!" Ramah called from the narrow hallway, her all-natural complexion glowing as she

159

smiled. "What are you doing out there? Come in, come in!"

The moment the screen door no longer acted as a barrier between them, Ramah wrapped Crystina in a motherly hug, squeezing her. "Come through, honey. You must be hungry. I've made plenty. Come in, come in. Sit down..."

She was led by hand down the narrow hallway, Chizzy on her heel, his paws clumsily scraping the floorboards.

"Look who I found on our doorstep!" Ramah announced.

Crystina's heartbeat quickened the moment she saw him. While his sisters raced to meet her and drag her to her long-empty seat, Jeremiah's jaw slackened.

Deb placed her beside Jeremiah and kissed her hair. "Girl, it has been *way* too long."

Crystina glanced between them. "No one sits here?"

"It's your seat," Isaac said, stuffing a roast potato in his mouth. He then pointed to the empty seat at the head of the long rustic table. "And that's dad's."

Crystina's heart swelled.

"I'll get you a plate," Milkie said, dancing her way to the kitchenette and back.

Viva leapt up next, her dreadlocks whipping through the air. "And I'll get you a drink. Juice, okay?"

"Actually, just water thanks," Crystina said. "I've been walking a while, so I'm a bit thirsty."

Jeremiah shifted beside her, seemingly uncertain of what to do with his large self. His leg started bouncing, the way it did when he was deep in thought, anxious, or frustrated. He bumped her leg.

"Sorry," he said beneath his breath.

"It's okay."

Tension brewed like a storm. She could feel it swelling and moving between them. An electric storm. She could feel the heat of him, hovering over the surface of his skin like an aura. So she was grateful when a plate with sausages and roasted vegetables appeared before her, anything to keep her mouth occupied from speaking.

Such a thing didn't restrict the Sanderson family, however, as they spoke over one another and each tried to fit a word into the conversation. All except for Jeremiah, who didn't seem interested in playing the game tonight.

"Mama, can I be excused to play with the dog outside?" Isaac finally asked. His plate just about licked clean.

"Only if you kiss your mama first."

He grinned, pushed back his chair then wrapped his lanky arms around her neck and smothered her cheek with kisses.

"Okay okay!" She laughed. "Go on. Go play."

He chuckled. "What's his name?"

"Melchizedek," Crystina and Jeremiah said at once.

Silence fell.

Deb's laugh exploded with juice spraying from her mouth and nose.

"Ew!" Milkie squealed.

"I'll get the paper towel," Viva said.

"It's Chizzy for short," Jeremiah said.

Ramah grinned. "Well, thank goodness for that."

"Come on, Chizzy," Isaac called, still laughing as he led the pup to the backyard.

Crystina chuckled to herself. She had forgotten how easy it was to be here. Then again, she wasn't the only visitor they'd had. Harper had visited and Ramah had welcomed her like a daughter too. Which left Crystina wondering—had Harper sat in her seat?

"Hey." Jeremiah gently nudged her with his elbow.

She swiftly pushed all thoughts of Harper from her mind. It wasn't healthy. And most importantly, it wasn't the reason God had told her to come here, of that she was certain.

So, playfully, she nudged him back.

He recoiled, holding his rib. "Argh!"

"*What?*"

Jeremiah laughed. "You don't know your own strength."

She shook her head, beaming. "Did you really think I'd fall for that?"

"Well, it made you smile, so it was totally worth it."

Her insides warmed and she glanced across the table to see Ramah smiling into her plate.

"Well, I have homework to do," Milkie said, rising from her chair. "Don't be a stranger, okay? Promise?"

Crystina nodded. "Sure."

"Yeah, come to think of it, Vee, I need your help with that... *thing*..." Deb said.

"What are you talking about?" Viva's brow furrowed. "I'm still eating, can't it wait—"

"No, it really can't." Deb grabbed her by the hand.

Viva scoffed one more mouthful before she was dragged from the table.

"Well, they're not known for their subtlety." Ramah patted her mouth with her napkin. "I've got to get to work anyway, I picked up an extra shift at the hospital." She floated over and kissed Crystina's hair. "It's so good to see you, sweetheart. I've missed you."

"I've missed you too," Crystina said softly, and she meant it. She had missed everything about this home. Though, one person probably more than the rest.

Finally alone, both Crystina and Jeremiah stared at their plates for a long moment, unmoving. Then, without looking up, Crystina slowly reached for his hand settled on his bouncing knee. His movement

163

stopped. Her hands were small, pale, and slender compared to his. Gently, she wove two fingers around his. He *was* warm. It was as though he exuded heat. She fought to steady her breath, but it came out shaky. She still hadn't looked up at him. Instead, she focused on the feeling of his skin against hers.

He took a loud breath then released it, shuddering.

When she eventually looked up at him, his dark eyes were glazed with suppressed tears.

"I wasn't sure if you'd ever want to see me again," he said.

She swallowed. Her mouth was dry. She would reach for her water, only she didn't want to break this moment.

"I'm so sorry. I didn't mean for any of this to happen," he said.

Crystina had to remember Abuela's advice. This was not about them. This was about the enemy trying to derail them from their callings and to steal their joy. The enemy had been running circles around Jeremiah for what seemed like a long time and enough was enough.

Jeremiah's fingers brushed hers gently.

Shivers sprang up from her hand all the way up her arm, but before she could allow herself to fall into this dream, she had to ask, "Why were you at the coffee shop with her?"

"She wanted to talk. And I finally agreed because I wanted her advice... about you."

"Me?"

"Yeah, well, before everything happened, she was the next person closest to you." He shrugged. "I didn't know what to do. I still don't..."

"Jerry," she began softly, "I don't want us to be like this. This awkwardness. And fighting? It's not us. I just... I want you to be honest with me."

"I felt guilty. I couldn't tell you, so I avoided you."

"I thought you were just busy studying all those months."

"Not always. Sometimes I just didn't want to lie to you."

Her hand wrapped around his tighter.

He squeezed. "I was so scared of losing you for good."

"You'll never lose me for good. Best friends, always and forever, remember?"

Jeremiah finally met her gaze. "But I can't just be friends with you." He blinked and a few stray tears fell. He let out a breathy bittersweet laugh and sniffled. "But I know I made a mistake... and I can't take it back... I wish I could."

A sickening feeling swelled in Crystina's core when she asked, "Did it happen more than once?"

"No."

She sighed, somewhat relieved, but there was still so much niggling at her, begging for more information.

"She showed up after one of her dad's big nights," he said. "She needed a place to crash. We were talking and I felt sorry for her... but after it happened, I just felt sick. I knew I'd ruined something good."

With her free hand, Crystina reached for her water and guzzled it down. Her neck was hot. Her mouth dry. Her heart racing. When she placed her empty glass down, she slipped her hand away from Jeremiah.

"You don't get it," she said softly. "Harper's perfect. I can't compete with that."

Jeremiah's face twisted, cringing against her words. "Wow, you really have no idea how beautiful you are."

"I just—"

"Chizzy totally did a dump in the yard!" Isaac announced from the backdoor.

Jeremiah glared at him.

"Never mind." His younger brother backed away. "I'll... er... clean it up, I guess..."

Jeremiah flashed a crooked grin.

Crystina laughed. "Talk about ruining the moment."

"Why, what would have happened if he hadn't come in?"

"Honestly? I probably would've asked you more uncomfortable questions."

"Such as?"

She swallowed all amusement. "How long are you going to keep running away from God?"

"Hmm, excellent question."

"Jerry, I'm serious."

He toyed with his fork for a moment. "So am I. In fact, I drafted my letter today." He exhaled hard. "To formally drop out of college."

"What?"

"I guess after seeing you at the coffee shop and thinking everything over... I didn't want to hear it the other day because I knew you were telling the truth. And I need you to tell the truth. I need you to tell me to pull my head in."

She smiled. "Well, I'm sure I can help you there."

"I guess, I just need you if I'm going to do this. You know, ruin my future..." He shook his head. "*Need* probably isn't the right word... What I need is Jesus to help me. But with you, I just—"

"*Want?*" she offered, then added in a small voice, "... me."

"Mmm."

She blinked up at him. "By the way, God totally told me to come here. It's the first time the Holy Spirit has spoken in days."

"Way to change the subject, Crystina." He laughed and squeezed her knee.

"I didn't mean to—" She placed her hand over his and brushed his knuckles. "What I mean is... this is good.

I just need you to be patient with me, okay? And I need you to be honest. Even if it's hard."

As he studied her face, hope ignited his eyes. "Crystina, what are you saying?"

She leaned closer, watching him to catch his reaction. "I want you too."

His mouth fell open.

Crystina's words hung in the air between them; the full meaning of them dawned afresh over her. A magnet in her soul drew her to him. She might have followed the pull had the sharp skid of the backdoor not sent her slamming her body back into the chair.

"Sorry, but he's done another dump." Isaac shook his head. "I reckon it's the leftover chicken Mama gave him."

Once again, Jeremiah glared at his younger brother.

"It's okay," Crystina said.

"It's not."

Hesitantly, she shifted away from the table. "I should probably take Chizzy home anyway."

Jeremiah pushed his chair back. "I'll walk you."

"No, it's fine, you stay. Study. How many times have I walked home from here?" She shrugged. "I'll be okay."

And with that, Crystina quietly escaped before she did something she might later regret.

CHAPTER 18

Spirit of Power

Hope set Crystina's heart ablaze. Courage rushed through her veins like a shot of adrenaline. This was where God wanted them. Vulnerable. Completely reliant on Him. Sensitive to their spiritual calling and purpose in His Kingdom work.

She walked briskly, excited to tell Abuela and yet nervous too. What would she think of her and Jerry? Crystina trusted Abuela's opinion and a slight doubt crept into her mind. What if she thought it was a bad idea? Could Crystina recant what had been said tonight? Surely after being so brazen at the kitchen table, nothing would be the same between them again. They both knew that the promise they held onto as friends had grown into something more, something deeper.

Chizzy toddled by her side. But as they crossed the esplanade, the pup barked and bared his teeth.

Crystina froze. Dread washed over her. She searched the darkness.

"Please Jesus... protect me..."

A chill crept over her. Chizzy growled from beside her and she stepped back toward the streetlamp. Heavy footsteps echoed her movements. An ominous presence loomed around her.

"Who's there?!"

A man stepped into view, cringing against the light. His broad body was shrouded in a black hooded jacket and his matted hair hung in clumps about his face. His stare held hers through dark narrow slits seemingly void of life. He wasn't blind, of that she was certain, for he watched her intensely.

Fear gripped her. Her heartbeat thudded, sending her body trembling. She opened her mouth to speak but all she could manage was the same whispered prayer.

"Please Jesus... protect me..."

The man took another step toward her, but Chizzy cut in front of her with a deep growl.

He huffed before returning his attention to her. With a low voice, he said. "You are causing trouble, Azure Blaze."

Crystina sucked in a breath. "Who are you?"

He shook his head, his hood overshadowing his face until it almost appeared as though he had no face at all. "Things will only get worse," he said. "You have been warned."

His warning was followed by the roar of the ocean, reminding her of what she had to lose and what she had already lost. Cold air threatened to breach the summer night with a veil of winter chill. It gripped her bones and left her feeling withered, weary, and weak. Before her emotions could consume her completely, she instinctively began to search her memory for a piece of Scripture to hold onto.

Don't be afraid.

Fear not.

Be courageous.

The Lord is your refuge.

Snippets flashed before her mind's eye. There was no reference to hold onto, but biblical phrases came to her in fevered bursts. Then, finally, the Holy Spirit brought 2 Timothy 1:7 to the forefront of her mind.

"For God has not given you a spirit of fear but of power and of love and a sound mind..."

And it was enough for her to straighten her shoulders, raise her chin, and remember who she was and Whose she was.

"God has not given me a spirit of fear," she said. The same strength from that night below the bridge came to her once again, a depth beyond her years seasoned her words with God's truth. "In Jesus, I have a spirit of power and love and a sound mind."

The man staggered back slightly.

Crystina stepped forward. "I have the Holy Spirit living inside of me and I am a daughter of the ever-living God..."

His filthy hands reached to cover his ears.

So Crystina raised her voice to a shout. "You have no place here! As a daughter of the Most High God I command you to leave in the name of Jesus Christ!"

He shrieked, cowering at the name she declared with such force. And suddenly, the eerie presence had faded, and the man was gone.

Awe filled her and she fell to her knees, overwhelmed by the power of the Holy Spirit within her, shaking as she recounted all that had just transpired. She had encountered an evil force. The enemy was after her. But she understood now what she'd only known before in theory. She already had all the weapons she needed in her spiritual arsenal, and in the powerful name of Jesus Christ, every knee would bow, and every evil flee.

CHAPTER 19

Jeremiah's Prayer

"And pray in the Spirit on all occasions with all kinds of prayers and requests. With this in mind, be alert and always keep on praying for all the Lord's people."
EPHESIANS 6:18

Four words was all it took to wring tears from Jeremiah.

"I want you too."

Then she had left too soon. Too soon for him to understand the capacity and the expectation of her want and the sense of direction of that want moving forward.

His mind tried to catch up to this new reality, but his heart was thumping too loud to string a coherent thought. Instead, his body surged, and instinct spurred him on to chase after her, to hold her and never let her go. But he had to be patient. By God's grace, he *would* be patient, because no matter what happened from this moment, he finally knew the truth. She wanted him too.

Everything was different now. This wasn't little Crystina Santos sneaking out to meet him for a late swim—something they had started doing to counter her fear of the water—this was his Crystina, the woman he wanted. The woman who wanted him in return. After tonight, nothing would be the same again. So after their goodnight, he waited a minute before making his own way down the path to the lighthouse. He just needed to know she was home safe. He couldn't explain it, but it was as though a magnet inside him was drawing him out toward the water to watch over her as she walked home. Then, strangely, Chizzy growled, and Crystina froze on the pavement by the streetlamp.

Jeremiah couldn't see anyone else, but he heard Crystina's voice. His pace quickened. Who was she talking to? Chizzy stood protectively beside her, his bared teeth gleaming in the moonlight. A supernaturally commanding voice came from her in a shout. Then she collapsed to her knees.

Jeremiah's feet rolled into a run. "Crystina!"

Within moments, he wrapped her in his arms. She was trembling. Her eyes squeezed shut.

"What's wrong? What happened?"

"There was a man..."

He looked around. "I didn't see anyone."

"That's... not possible."

"I was following you," he said gently. "I wanted to make sure you got home safe."

She peered up at him. "What?"

"Crystina, there was no one there."

"But he knew I was Azure Blaze. He said I was causing trouble!"

Shivers exploded down his arms, and he felt cold. Yet, an unfamiliar fire blazed in his spirit, and he drew her to him again, holding her protectively. "What do you need? What can I do?"

"Chizzy needs to go home..."

"Crystina." He cupped her chin in his hands. "What do you need?"

"Could you take me to St Peter's cathedral?"

He knew it wasn't the time to ask questions. "Of course."

"I can explain on the way. There's still so much you don't know."

Once Chizzy was home with Abuela, Jeremiah drove in silence, listening while Crystina told him of JCPD and the women of St Peter's who had been targeted. He tried not to let jealousy distract him when she told him Xavier knew she was Azure Blaze. Now was not the time for petty feelings, especially after the news Crystina had learned today. It was a miracle she still wanted him. He couldn't sabotage this new season of their lives, especially when she had accepted him and his flaws so selflessly.

"So, when are you going to send the letter?" Crystina asked as they pulled into the gravel carpark of St Peter's.

"Way to change the subject." He gave her hand a brief squeeze. "After I tell Mom, I guess. I feel like I owe her that much after everything we've all been through."

"She'll understand."

"Yeah, I was going to tell her tonight."

Crystina's face dropped. "But I gatecrashed?"

"Technically... but I'm glad you did." He switched off the ignition. "Come on, let's head inside."

When Crystina rounded the car, Jeremiah took her hand before approaching the front door. It was slightly ajar as though someone was expecting them. Then again, on yet another balmy summer night, it could have just been for airflow.

St Peter's was quiet except for the crackle of burning wicks. The Watchman prayed silently in the front pew. Candlelight softened his features and must have made it impossible for him to see them approach with his poor eyesight. Still, he didn't seem to be surprised by their presence, only concerned.

His brow creases deepened. "How can I help?"

Jeremiah then listened when Crystina relayed her story to the Watchman in the sacred safety of St Peter's cathedral. The priest listened intently, seemingly unsurprised when she spoke of her supernatural alias.

"So this man," the Watchman began, "he knew you were Azure Blaze?"

"Yes."

"And you have never seen him before?"

"No, I would remember. He had long unkept hair, and dark features, and clothes. And his eyes just looked... empty. Not like he was blind—" She winced. "Sorry. I just mean, there was no life in them."

He nodded thoughtfully.

Anger simmered beneath Jeremiah's skin as he listened. He wanted answers; for Crystina but also for himself. How could he protect her if he didn't know who or what she needed protection from?

"What do you think it means?" Jeremiah asked.

"I think he may be right, she is causing trouble," the Watchman said, turning to face Crystina. "You are causing trouble in the spiritual realm, and the enemy does not like the fact that the people of Juniper City are beginning to question whether there is a God. For so long, they have just accepted their lives as they are, but now you are true evidence of what intimacy with Christ can look like. You are living proof that the Holy Spirit can minister to us in tangible ways. My child, your faith has caused others to doubt their unbelief."

Crystina nodded slowly. "Our battle is not against flesh and blood..."

"Did you partake in the sacraments this morning?" the Watchman asked.

Jeremiah watched Crystina, awaiting her response. What sort of question was that? Did she really—

"Not today," she said, glancing up at Jeremiah. "It has been a rough couple of days. I slept in..."

The Watchman nodded slowly as he approached the altar. He removed a golden dome to reveal an ornate goblet and a rustic loaf dusted with flour.

"You need to." He stared blankly in their direction. "Both of you. Because if you are going to continue on this journey, then you will need more spiritual sustenance than you are receiving. Mass will not sustain you. Morning prayer will not sustain you. A verse a day to keep the enemy at bay, will not sustain you."

"I read more than—" Jeremiah began to defend himself but, for the first time, the Watchman's eyes fixed on him. It was as though he could see through his soul.

"You must be reminded of the covenant the Lord our God made with Abraham, Isaac, and Jacob," the Watchman said. "You must be reminded of the new covenant purchased through the blood of Jesus Christ. You must understand why you take up this cross daily and follow Him."

Shivers burned down his spine. Jeremiah glanced at the altar then to Crystina then back to the Watchman. "And communion will do that?"

"It is a start," he said, "and as the spiritual leader, you must be fervent in praying for Azure Blaze. Can you do that?"

Guilt overwhelmed Jeremiah. In all his wrestling with God lately and his calling and his feelings for Crystina, when had he stopped to really pray for her? And what did the Watchman mean by calling him the 'spiritual leader'? He and Crystina weren't exactly in a relationship yet. Were they?

The Watchman held out his hand, not for Crystina, but for Jeremiah. "Come," he said, "it is time."

Jeremiah had no idea what the Watchman meant but he knew better than to stay where he was. So he approached the altar and stood at the lectern, leaning over its heavy Bible. He read aloud from the gospel of Mark.

"And as they were eating, Jesus took bread, blessed and broke it, and gave it to them and said, 'Take, eat; this is My body.' Then He took the cup, and when He had given thanks He gave it to them, and they all drank from it. And He said to them, 'This is My blood of the new covenant, which is shed for many...'"

Then, Jeremiah broke the bread and they both ate. He and Crystina then sipped the wine and paused to remember the new covenant.

In his heart, Jeremiah prayed for protection over Crystina, over Azure Blaze. He then made a vow and asked the Holy Spirit to keep him accountable. From this evening forward, so long as it was within his power to do so, he would remember, as often as he did this, in remembrance of Jesus. For as often as he ate the bread and drank the cup, he proclaimed the Lord's death till He returned.

Jeremiah turned the thick antiquated pages to the book of Psalms. Then he laid one hand on Crystina's shoulder. In this moment of reverence, standing in the presence of almighty God, he prayed over her again. Only this time, he prayed scripture over her, and he prayed it out loud.

"*Whoever dwells in the shelter of the Most High will rest in the shadow of the Almighty. I will say of the Lord, 'He is my refuge and my fortress, my God, in whom I trust.' Surely he will save you from the fowler's snare and from the deadly pestilence. He will cover you with his feathers, and under his wings you will find refuge; his faithfulness will be your shield and rampart. You will not fear the terror of night, nor the arrow that flies by day, nor the pestilence that stalks in the darkness, nor the plague that destroys at midday. A thousand may fall at your side, ten thousand at your right hand, but it will not come near you. You will only observe with your eyes and see the punishment of the wicked.*" His voice strengthened. "*If you say, 'The Lord is my refuge,' and you make the Most High your dwelling, no harm will overtake you, no disaster will come near your tent. For he will command his angels concerning you to guard you in all your ways; they will lift you up in their hands, so that you will not strike your foot against a stone.*" His hand slammed the lectern as the presence of the Spirit of God filled him. "*You will tread on the lion and the cobra; you will trample the great lion and the serpent.*" Then, somehow, like a slip of the tongue or a slight of hand, Jeremiah saw her name written in the Word of God. "*'Because Crystina loves me,' says the Lord, 'I will rescue her; I will protect her, for she acknowledges my name. She will call on me, and I will answer her; I will be with her in trouble, I will deliver her and honor her. With long life I will satisfy her and show her my salvation.*"

When Jeremiah finally looked up from God's Word, tears streamed down Crystina's cheeks.

"The Lord is my refuge..." She gasped back a sob then buried her face into his chest.

Jeremiah held her, hand in her hair, his arm wrapped protectively around her. She was so close he could feel her heart thumping against his chest. Or was it his own? He didn't know any more.

"We have to keep praying." Crystina pressed her forehead to his chest. "Every day. Promise me. We have to hold onto this..."

His lips brushed her head before he rested his cheek on her hair. "Always and forever. I promise. We'll pray every day."

"We'll pray for protection," she whispered. "Promise me."

His arms tightened around her. He desperately wanted to tug her back and gaze into her face, to find the answers written there even if they didn't come out in word form. But he didn't trust himself. At least here, in this intimate moment, he could create enough distance between their mouths to keep the temptation from becoming unbearable.

"I can't lose you," she said at last. "I just can't..."

"You won't."

"You don't know that. We don't know anything."

"That's not true," he said. "We know God is for us. And we know that right now, this moment, is a gift. We know that we have victory through Jesus Christ. And we know that we both have a calling on our lives that we have to live up to." He sighed. "But we know the Holy Spirit will help us."

"Even so," she said softly. "You have to be safe, okay? I can't lose you. Not now..."

Jeremiah nodded against her and in his heart, he finished her sentence.

"Not now that we're together."

But neither of them seemed prepared to say those words out loud.

CHAPTER 20

Nightmares

For the first time since she was a child, Crystina dreamt of the accident. She dreamt of the icy water beyond Juniper Bay, of the blackness as far as she could see. Then, blinding white. The beam of light from the beacon made its rotation. Her eyes were constantly squinting. Adjusting. Her frozen fingers clung to the adult life vest that was too big for her childish frame. She tried to blow the whistle, but she was so far from shore, she didn't know if anyone would hear. It had all happened so quickly. One moment they were enjoying Juniper City's fireworks and the next Jacob had been lighting his own. It was meant to be all in good fun. No one knew he even had fireworks in that old backpack. At just thirteen, Jacob had changed schools and mixed in with the wrong crowd. Some people called them misunderstood, others called them troublemakers, but Jacob had found them fascinating with their unconventional upbringings. Matthew, only eight years old, called out for Dad. Anthony, two years his senior, shushed him. Crystina backed away from her brothers, scared of the flame her eldest brother wielded. Mama's scream still rang in her ears as Crystina's footing failed and she backed up and over the railing. Frozen water met her fall, though the inflated vest at least kept her buoyant. Then, before she knew it, fireworks exploded before her eyes. A ball of fire consumed the boat. The force pushed her into the water, but she clung to the oversized life vest until it brought her bobbling to the surface. Mama had insisted she wear the life vest inflated. It had been uncomfortable, but it was the only way Mama said she was getting on that boat. Abuela had agreed with the decision before she and Papi went to bed early. It was Crystina's first New Year's celebration, and it would be her last. She never wanted to celebrate the New Year again. Not after this one had stolen so much.

But her dream hadn't stopped there. This time there was someone else on the boat.

Jeremiah.

He held her stare until the boat was aflame and then he was lost to the ocean along with her family.

Her grown self then floated in that water, screaming against the frosted wind, begging someone to hear her. She should have died. In the dead of winter, in the middle of the night, a scrawny six-year-old shouldn't have survived those waters.

But she did.

"Jeremiah!" she screamed, launching upright in her bed. Chills slithered down her spine as she woke drenched in sweat.

Abuela stumbled into her room moments later, her arms outstretched. "Crystina, what's wrong?"

Crystina sobbed into her.

"Sshh, it's alright." She smoothed Crystina's damp hair. "It was a dream. It was just a dream."

But it had felt so real.

"You have not given me a spirit of fear," Crystina whispered over herself, "but of power, love, and a sound mind."

While Abuela rocked her, Crystina repeated 2 Timothy 1:7 over herself until it began to touch the deepest part of her soul. God had not given her a spirit of fear and if it didn't come from Him then it came from the enemy; the enemy who was set on derailing, distracting, and devastating her.

She tugged herself from Abuela and threw back the quilt to find her phone. She punched in the number she knew by heart.

"Crystina?"

She released a heavy sigh, weighted in fear. His voice soothed her soul. "You're okay."

"Of course, I'm okay."

"I dreamt of the accident. Only this time, you were there. You need to pray, Jerry. You need to pray over yourself too, not just me. Do you promise? Pray for protection over yourself."

"Crystina, calm down. I'm coming over."

"No, no." She cringed against the phone. "It's okay. I'm okay, it's just... Just be careful today, okay? I know you have to study..."

"No, I don't... I spoke to Mama last night after her shift. It's official, I'm dropping out."

"I'm sorry." She quickly collected herself. "I know that must have been hard."

"I'll jump in the shower and then I'll come straight there, okay?"

Her cheeks warmed and she slouched against her bookcase. "Yeah, sounds great. Thank you."

"Yeah, I'll really be doing you a favor... Getting to spend more time with my favorite person. It's a tough gig but someone's gotta do it."

A smile tugged on her lips as she heard him crank the faucet.

"Better go before I take you in the shower with me—"

A nervous laugh bubbled out of Crystina.

"I didn't mean that the way it sounded." He chuckled down the phone. "Abuela's not there is she?"

"Yeah, yeah, she is." She smiled against the phone then whispered, "but lucky for you you're not on speaker."

"And she's old so her hearing's not great."

Crystina rolled her eyes. "Go have a shower."

"I'm going!" There was a smile in his voice. *"See you soon."*

She shook her head and tried to suppress her grin from consuming her whole face.

"I'll start breakfast," Abuela said, rising from the bed. "But you can tell Jeremiah, my hearing is just fine."

Crystina bit her lip and sent a brief text. *"She heard you."*

She then dropped her phone on the bed and pulled her Bible onto her lap. It fell open to Psalm 118. So she soaked it in, reading it over until the words cemented themselves in her soul. It was Abuela who had instilled a love of God's Word in her. A prayer warrior for a grandmother had been one of God's greatest gifts in Crystina's life.

By the time Jeremiah stood sheepishly on the doorstep, toolbox in hand, Abuela had prepared communion for them with three of Papi's antique shot glasses instead of two.

Then while Crystina showered and dressed, Jeremiah set to work on the weather-beaten front door. Chizzy kept him company and Abuela made espresso.

When Crystina finally emerged into the living room with her best dress pants and shirt, she reached for her motorcycle gear. She slipped the armored pants on over her work uniform and zipped up her jacket.

Abuela stared at her. "You're riding today?"

Crystina paused. "I feel like the Holy Spirit told me to. Oh, but before I forget..." She reached up around her neck to undo the clasp of her necklace. She then held it out for Jeremiah.

He glanced at the sapphire crucifix then back to her. "Thanks, but it's really not my style."

"Put it somewhere on your body," she said. "I don't mind where."

Even with his deep chocolate skin, she saw Jeremiah's blush. "If you insist."

"I do."

He took the pendant, but his eye contact never wavered. Their hands magnetized to each other during the exchange, and those two words hung between them like a promise.

Crystina left the lighthouse and arrived at Legion International Media as Azure Blaze. Weaving between the banked-up traffic, she pulled her bike up onto the pavement and cut the engine. Police tape surrounded the building, crowds were barricaded, and police officers littered the street and beyond the floor-to-ceiling glass windows of the building's ground floor.

"Why did you leave your burner phone at home?" Kendra demanded.

"How did you know—"

"Never mind, you're here now."

"What's going on?" Crystina asked, reaching for her helmet.

"Leave that on for now, Azure Blaze, and come with me."

Kendra nodded to an officer who released the tape and allowed Crystina access. In the distance, she caught a glimpse of Xavier amid a huddle of employees. Harper watched from a distance and Crystina couldn't help but wonder if she recognized her. Once inside, Kendra led Crystina to the ground floor ladies' room where she pulled out her gun and shot the overhead security camera.

Crystina jumped. "What was that for?"

Kendra secured her gun once more. "You can take your helmet off now."

Slowly, Crystina obeyed.

"I assume you know Emma Dunkirk?"

"Yes, of course."

"She's missing. I understand she also attends St Peters?"

Dread descended on Crystina.

"Xavier received a threat this morning," Kendra went on, "an anonymous letter saying to give up the identity of Azure Blaze, or..."

She swallowed hard. "It's because she wrote the article on me."

Kendra folded her arms. "That's why we assume she was taken."

"But she didn't know who I was."

"Something the kidnapper wasn't counting on. Is there anything you can tell us about Emma?"

"She's a fan." Crystina shrugged hopelessly. "We've been work buddies, I suppose, but I don't know much about her except her love for journalism. That's why I contacted her as Azure Blaze. I was hoping it would get her noticed..."

"Don't do that," Kendra said sternly. "This is not your fault. Some sick person has got an idea into their head. That's all."

"But Emma is missing? She could be—"

She shook her head. "It would be foolish for the assailant to harm her. It would ruin any leverage."

Well, that was something. "Okay, what do you need me to do?"

"Honestly? I can't believe I'm even saying this, but..."

"What?"

"Azure Blaze, I need you to pray." Kendra's fierce stare burned into her. "I need you to find out where she is."

"Do you believe He'll tell me?" Crystina asked softly.

"I believe He *can* tell you. I don't know if He *will*, He's God. And I pray that if I have any unbelief that He would help me to believe. But yes, I believe, in my heart, that He *wants* to tell you. If only to show daughters like me who haven't stepped foot in a church since Christmas, that He is real and He is there."

Crystina sucked in a breath.

"But remember, Azure Blaze, time is not on our side. The demand is an exclusive on your identity on all media outlets under Legion International Media first thing tomorrow morning and a recant on your claims to be 'Spirit-led'. Claim it was all a hoax, that you fooled Juniper City. That Azure Blaze is a joke, basically."

Kendra cleared her throat. "Look, I can't tell you what to do, but Emma has already been missing for well over twenty-four hours. It's not looking good."

Crystina thought of Emma's goofy snort, her incidental meerkat impersonation, the way she had written so faithfully to all Crystina had told her. How could someone even contemplate hurting a person like her?

"So what if we *do* release an exclusive?"

"Azure Blaze," she said slowly, "a nurse has been attacked after her shift. A young woman had been drugged and taken to a remote property and probably would be dead if it wasn't for the Spirit of God guiding you there and consequently leading *us* there. A baby was in a stolen car that you literally had to jump in to stop.

And now, one of your colleagues is missing and the person behind this wants to know your identity. Call me crazy, but I'm thinking we shouldn't negotiate with this terrorist. We simply have to find another way."

On the outside, Crystina nodded her agreement, but inside, she was torn. *She* was the one the kidnapper wanted, not Emma. She didn't know if it was the fluorescent lighting or the sterile stench of bleach, but clarity seemed to overwhelm her. This wasn't the time to hide behind her helmet. But neither was this the time to bend to the whims of the enemy. No, this battle would need to be on the terms of One, and One alone—Jesus. He would determine the outcome, and she knew that ultimately, He was victorious.

"Azure Blaze?" Kendra stared her down. "I'm not going to say this twice. Don't do anything stupid."

She remained silent.

Kendra reduced her voice to a whisper. "Promise me—"

"When hard pressed, I cried to the LORD," Crystina began softly, reciting the words she had read that morning from Psalm 118 and had repeated over and over herself as a prayer. *"He brought me into a spacious place."* She met Kendra's gaze. *"The LORD is with me; I will not be afraid. What can mere mortals do to me?"*

"Plenty!" Kendra shouted.

Serenity washed over Crystina's face. *"The LORD is with me; He is my helper. I look in triumph on my enemies."*

Kendra took hold of her shoulders. "You won't be looking at anyone if you're dead."

"*It is better to take refuge in the LORD than to trust in humans... than to trust in princes...*"

"Azure Blaze. I'm warning you—"

"*All the nations surrounded me, but in the name of the LORD I cut them down. They surrounded me on every side, but in the name of the LORD—*" Crystina paused, her jaw clenched. "*I. Cut. Them. Down.*"

Kendra backed away. "You have a death wish if you reveal yourself!"

"*The LORD is my strength and my defense. He has become my salvation,*" Crystina declared. "*I will not die but live, and will proclaim what the LORD has done.*"

"If you do this," Kendra said, "you're on your own."

Like Father, Like...

Holy Spirit fueled adrenaline coursed through Crystina's veins. She powered through Legion International Media with such determination that no officer thought to stop her. She was on a mission for answers and by the grace of God, she prayed she'd find them.

"Please, Lord," she whispered beneath her breath as she punched the elevator button. "Please help me..."

An empty workspace greeted her. She marched past her cramped old desk nestled beside the identical one where Emma had worked before 'opportunity' had led to disaster. But Crystina couldn't focus on that right now. Looking back wouldn't help Emma and, if Kendra was right about anything, it was the fact that whoever was behind this had a diseased mind.

Whispering prayers in a tongue only God understood, Crystina made her way to the large corner office she'd sat in so many times. Only, this time, she claimed Xavier's chair. He had to have been thrown out in a hurry because his computer wasn't locked. She glanced down through the wide glass window to see him and the remainder of Legion International Media employees still contained behind tape. Then she set to work. She opened folder after folder. Checked the recycle bin. Then went to his emails. Countless emails flooded the inbox. She scrolled until she found an unread thread. It had been sent that morning but remained untouched, its subject line in bold black text: PLANS.

Amos,
Refer to attached plans for the Legion Hotel.
Regards,
Lee Bernard

Lee Bernard? The CEO of Legion International Media? She hadn't ever seen him in the office and assumed he could even be a myth. Crystina supposed it was none of her concern, should he decide to branch into the hotel business. That was until she opened the attachment. She knew that place too well. For the

Legion Hotel was drafted to stand between the iron and glass of old Juniper town. Three words were written in neat blue pen over the scanned document: *"Revival is here!"*

Lee Bernard wanted to revive old Juniper town, and he wanted the land of St Peter's cathedral to do it.

Next, Crystina scrolled through the folders in Xavier's inbox and found one with the letters 'LS'. Clicking it open, she found an array of emails describing the intimidation tactics for St Peters. She continued to scroll, her eyes quickly scanning the plot to scare the priest out of Juniper all together. The way they strategically chose the females who would have the most emotional pull on the congregation. She found one email describing their disappointment over the anonymous donation.

The infant was perhaps the most disturbing of all. She belonged to the substitute preacher who was standing in until the Watchman was officially ordained. The mother whom Crystina had helped that night had been the preacher's wife. Every attack was calculated and planned to perfection to destroy the congregation of St Peter's. What they hadn't counted on, however, was the God of the universe reaching out to His people through the most unlikely means.

Her.

'Azure Blaze' began to emerge in the email trail with Lee Bernard describing her as a nuisance. The last email sent to Lee Bernard, however, read:

I know who she is.
I'll take care of it.
Amos.

To which Lee Bernard replied:

Good.
I'm proud of you, Son.

Crystina's mind swirled. Her mouth went dry as she tried to focus on the words before her. Was it a term of affection? Or was he Lee Bernard's son? Xavier said he barely knew his father, that he was on the board of directors of the Juniper City Police Department?

She opened Xavier's browser and searched 'Lee Bernard'. His impressive profile came up immediately and she scanned his list of credentials. There it was— CEO of Legion International Media and on the board of directors of the Juniper City Police Department. He was also on a handful of committees, including that of the St Peter's church council.

"What?"

"Santos, I'm disappointed in you," Xavier said from the doorway.

She looked up and keen fear reignited every ounce of adrenaline in her body.

"I even took the time to get you a coffee." He placed it down on the desk, it had the same smiley face and "S" scrawled on the lid.

Please, Jesus, help me...

He leaned over the desk and pressed the button that turned the glass walls opaque. "Now," he said, "let's have a little chat."

"Why have you been helping me?"

He leaned back into the guest chair. "You know what they say. Keep your friends close and all that..."

She blinked back the sheen over her eyes.

He groaned. "You're not going to cry again, are you?"

"You hired me to be your personal assistant? You brought flowers and... coffee..."

"What, you didn't think I actually liked you, did you?"

She felt herself shrink in his chair. "Where's Emma? You know who I am. Why demand I reveal myself when you could have done it all along? Why send yourself a letter at all?"

"You really are stupid, aren't you?" He chuckled. "I have to keep my hands clean, Santos. If I announced that I knew who you were, all eyes would be on me. This way all they see is this pathetic little girl. The whole of Juniper City will be rid of this enigmatic picture of a heroine you've painted and will see you for what you truly are. You're just a scared little orphan girl with an imaginary friend. You hear voices in your head. By the time I've finished with you, they'd be locking you up in a mental institution. You might as well have died with your family that night."

She searched his cool demeanor for any sense of the Amos Xavier she knew but found nothing. "Who *are* you?"

"Amos Bernard," he said with a tight smile. "Pleasure."

Her breath caught in her chest.

"It is one thing to bring cheap hope," he went on. "But to then take it away, to show Juniper City how ridiculous they were to put any faith in you, let alone in God... well, that will have them *hating* the church and all it represents. There is far too much toleration in our society. This way, once Emma publishes her new article renouncing all she had written, no one will believe in any higher power. It will all just be one big joke."

"Where's Emma?"

"Well, she's not dead yet. Neither is your Abuela. Or Jonah... no, Jerry, right? He's at the lighthouse today, isn't he? Ever the hero..."

Crystina swallowed hard. *Jesus, where are You? Help me! I've been following Your call on my life. How could it amount to this?*

"What do you want?" she asked, though instantly feared his response.

"I thought you'd never ask."

He grabbed her wrist and jerked her to her feet.

She stumbled after him. *Jesus. Please. Help me.*

"You'll say exactly what I tell you to," he growled and pulled her along. "I'm warning you, *Azure Blaze*. I made you. And I can destroy you."

Crystina couldn't help but think of Jeremiah and all the things left unsaid. All the things left undone. Here she had been so desperately worried for his safety, she hadn't stopped to consider her own. She wondered if there was more significance than she allowed herself to believe when she handed that crucifix over to him, making him promise to keep it on his person. How she longed to reach for it now and feel its tangible comfort. Instead, she would have to search within for the Ultimate Comforter, for the Spirit of God that had been so alive in her but whose voice was being drowned out by fear.

"You have not given me a spirit of fear," she whispered from between gritted teeth, "but of power, love, and self-control."

Xavier spun round. "What did you say?!"

"You didn't 'make' me. Jesus did." Crystina yanked her hand back. Bracing herself, she forced her palm into his chin as hard as she could and followed through with a kick in his groin.

Xavier flew back, cursing beneath his breath. When he staggered forward, she turned, switched feet, and pivoted into a back kick.

She turned to run but he snagged her ankle, pulling her to the floor.

"Not so fast."

He forced her onto her back then loomed over her, panting in her face. Crystina screamed until she felt the full force of his fist dislodge her jaw. Pain throbbed through her head, pounding in every direction. He swung his arm back again.

Bang.

A single bullet pierced the air.

Xavier screamed. He collapsed on top of her, his face scrunched in agony.

Crystina gasped for breath, desperate to focus on something, anything but the scent of blood filling her nostrils.

Kendra cocked her gun and held it to his temple.

Crystina's eyes grew round. A long moment continued to draw out between them. Kendra's fierce eyes. Xavier's screams. His bloodied thigh. Crystina's stare locked on the gun threatening to destroy his life.

"Kendra!" she mustered. "Kendra, stop!"

The fury in those dark eyes dissipated. Xavier's head hung forward. Kendra retracted, stowed her gun in the back of her jeans and heaved Xavier's body from Crystina. She then clicked her radio. "Medic on level three." Kendra reached for Crystina and helped her to her feet. "I told you not to do anything foolish, Azure Blaze."

Crystina doubled over, wincing as the vision overcame her mind. A gust of wind blew through the office as the Spirit of God filled the room. It was more powerful than she had ever experienced.

Then she saw it clearly.

Crystina had never realized how slow an elevator could be until she finally reached the ground level and sprinted toward her bike. Employees were still subdued on the pavement outside the building, seemingly restless until she emerged. Then a genuine applause staggered from the crowd. She wrung the throttle till the bike launched forward into the traffic, followed by cheers. She followed the familiar road she now knew by heart to the once forgotten bridge of old Juniper town.

CHAPTER 22

Fanning Into Flame

Emma was slumped by a pillar beneath the bridge, her long matted hair dangling before her. Straps and cords held her in place and the blue light of the computer on her lap washed over her pale face. One hand was strapped to her side while the other arm was restricted but her hand free to reach the alphabetical keys.

"Emma?!"

Slowly, she swung her head upwards. Disbelief turned to the purest joy as she gazed at Crystina. "It was you! All along, it was you!"

Crystina started to go to her but Kendra grasped her shoulder.

"Let me go," Crystina said.

"Azure Blaze," she warned, "she's connected to a bomb."

Panic set in. *No, Jesus. No...*

"She's right." All joy drained from Emma's face. "She's right. Stay where you are. All I have to do is press a button to submit the story, but I won't do it."

"Just do it, it doesn't matter," Crystina said. "Please."

"I'm calling back up," Kendra said, stepping away with her phone.

"You don't understand," Emma said, looking at Crystina. "This article renounces everything I said in the first one. It calls you crazy. It says God isn't real!"

Crystina paused. How could they do this? To Emma? To her? To Juniper City? How could Legion International Media have that much power to wield against them?

"How long do we have?" Crystina asked softly.

"Till 9am tomorrow. Then, regardless, Legion will have their exclusive. Either me, or Lee Bernard will be giving a statement about Amos Xavier being behind it all. Either way, he wins."

"No." Crystina sunk to her knees. "No matter what, God wins. Jesus has already won the victory over Satan, sin, and death. No matter what happens, He is still Sovereign. There is nothing happening in this moment He doesn't know."

Tears escaped down Emma's cheeks. "I rededicated my life to Christ on Sunday. I just wish I'd had longer to..."

"Don't talk like that. Kendra is a gun. She'll find someone who can fix this." Crystina gestured to the tapestry of cords holding her fast to the pillar. "She will."

"I'm glad I found out it was you before I die," she said. "You have inspired me so much. I wish we could've been friends."

"We *are* friends." Crystina reached for her but her arms fell short. "I'm just sorry I've been so caught up in my own world."

"It's a pretty exciting world," she said, "the world of Azure Blaze. I feel honored to have played any part in it."

"Emma..."

"I mean it, Crystina." She nodded. "Even if the police can't fix this, I will never regret it. And I know I don't have to fear death because Jesus will meet me on the other side."

"This isn't fair... *Please*, Jesus," She begged the sky. "Please. This isn't fair!"

"Will you do something for me?" Emma asked, glancing out into the darkness.

The light of the beacon suddenly lit their surroundings as it began its rotation. It had to be

Jeremiah. Just another small mercy. God telling her he was safe.

"Anything," Crystina said.

"Can I dictate an article to you? I have a blog that has got a crazy amount of followers since that first article. I want you to have the log-in details. I want you to keep the story going."

"Of course. What's the blog about?"

She shrugged. "*You.*"

Crystina's throat thickened.

"Well, Azure Blaze." She blinked away tears. "And that's you. It's always been you. I should've known."

Crystina smeared her nose with her sleeve then pulled out her phone and settled cross-legged on the concrete. "Okay, let's do this before we're both crying."

As the evening went on, Emma dictated, and Crystina typed into her phone. JCPD squads surrounded them, every officer wearing a heavily padded vest. Old Juniper Town hospital was evacuated, and patients moved to the Juniper City Hospital. A wide perimeter was set inside which only Emma, Crystina, Kendra, and a few from her specialist team remained. While Emma continued to dictate, sometimes correcting herself, two explosive experts focused on deciphering the cords and assessing the clock. Hours passed like mere minutes and again and again Crystina read back to Emma the words she herself had penned by dictation.

Crystina occasionally looked over to watch the concentration on the faces of the expert team, the beads of sweat forming on their brows, their eyes squinting in the glow of the flashlight.

"Azure Blaze is bringing the revival fire of the Holy Spirit to Juniper City," Emma said, her gaze fixed on Crystina as she typed. "God called her to this life because—"

Crystina's thumbs paused. Waiting.

"He chose her. It is as simple and as complicated as that. We may never understand why Azure Blaze was ignited in Juniper City but we don't have to. We just have to trust that the Lord knows what He's doing."

Crystina began to sob.

"And He is Sovereign." She winked at Crystina through her tears. "No power house CEO can change that. In fact, the darkness in this city only makes the light of the flame shine all the more bright." She gulped. "Tomorrow, I may not be here..."

Crystina's thumbs came to a halt.

"Tomorrow I may not be here," Emma repeated, nodding for Crystina to continue. "Tomorrow I may not be here, but I trust that you will take this revival fire and spread it through the city. Don't allow yourself to be bullied or dictated to—pun intended." She smiled. "Don't forget Who is in control. It's not who you see. It's not the enemy's puppets, for that is all they are. No, the

Lord Jesus Christ is King and He will reign forever and ever. Amen."

She swiftly finished off the final letters then watched Emma's face change to an expression of overwhelming peace. "They can't do it, can they?"

Kendra's fierce stare burned into her. "They will keep trying."

"No," Emma said. "You all have to get to safety. Go."

The two men looked at each other then up to Kendra, who nodded once.

"Azure Blaze." Kendra looked to the horizon. "It's time to go."

But Crystina's attention was fixed on Emma. "I can't leave you here. He'll save you. He *has* to."

Emma shook her head. "Azure Blaze," she began affectionately, "you and I both know, this message will be stronger if He doesn't."

Crystina gasped back her sobs.

"Go," Emma said.

Slowly, Crystina staggered to her feet.

"Oh, and guess what." Emma smiled. "I get to meet Him soon..."

"Then I'll see you there." Crystina started to back away. "I'll meet you by the Crystal Sea."

"Take your time," Emma said, "I know you're busy."

Crystina turned then spun to face her once more. "This is crazy, you know that, right?"

Emma nodded and smiled through her tears. "Go."

Kendra took Crystina's arms and led her to the next street where a paneled van waited. "In here."

Crystina followed the specialist team into the van and watched as each of them slumped into their seats. They had almost reached Juniper Bay when an explosion consumed the distant bridge and half of old Juniper town.

"Emma," Crystina whispered. "Lord, she's with You, now."

"I can't help but think this is what Legion wanted all along," Kendra said. "Old Juniper town flattened."

Crystina glanced down at her phone. "Maybe. But they won't be able to stop the revival fire Emma has started."

"She didn't start it. God did." Kendra said then added, "But she *did* fan it into flame."

CHAPTER 23

Smoke & Mirrors

"For now we see only a reflection as in a mirror; then we shall see face to face. Now I know in part; then I shall know fully, even as I am fully known."

1 CORINTHIANS 13:12

Jeremiah watched as smoke and ash rained down on Juniper Bay. He had spent the night in the lantern room. Waiting. But Crystina had never showed.

Now, in the blazing daylight of summer, a black van pulled up the gravel drive. With the sliding of the side door, stumbled Crystina. No motorbike. No helmet. Her armored jacket hung open over yesterday's shirt and even from this height, he could tell she had been crying.

He swiftly descended the spiral staircase and burst out the front door. Abuela staggered after him followed by Chizzy. On the patch of lawn by the cliffs, Crystina fell into Abuela's embrace and lingered there. Jeremiah watched on helplessly. His arms ached to hold her. The news had little to no information on the evacuation of old Juniper town. It seemed whatever had happened was being meticulously covered up.

Finally, Abuela released Crystina and Jeremiah stepped forward. He frowned as he took in her weathered appearance, his attention zeroing in on the deep bruising along her jaw. After her ordeal, he had expected her to freefall into his arms, to find relief and security there. Instead, he had to go to her, and she remained rigid.

"What's wrong?" he whispered.

She flinched back. "Nothing. It's just been a rough night."

He nodded and stepped away. Confusion overwhelmed him. What had changed between them?

"Come inside," Abuela said softly and guided Crystina toward the door.

Jeremiah hoped she might have noticed the way it effortlessly opened for her, but she was too distracted, too much in her own head. He wasn't sure whether to follow her inside or quietly slip away and wait until she wanted to talk.

Then Crystina said over her shoulder, "You coming?"

"Sure thing."

Abuela put the kettle on and Crystina went straight upstairs to take a shower.

"Did she say anything?" Jeremiah asked.

Abuela shook her head. "She's behaving very unusual."

"It has to be about that explosion in old Juniper town."

He sat at the family table, his knee bouncing, his gaze absentmindedly drifting to the television set. *Amos Xavier in hospital in stable condition after resisting arrest for fraud and miscellaneous crimes against the state of Juniper.* Legion International Media's C.E.O. Lee Bernard gave a statement, explaining how he was completely unaware of the lengths Xavier was willing to go to secure the property of St Peter's church for his hotel project. *He acted alone, Bernard said. I happen to be on the board of the St Peter's church and I am appalled that someone would target members of their congregation in such a way to intimidate the church into closing and selling their land.*

"Turn that off." Crystina marched through the living area in her sweats then plonked her laptop down on the kitchen table. "It's all lies."

"What are you doing?" Jeremiah asked.

She typed wildly, not looking up when she answered, "Telling the truth."

212

He peered over her shoulder. A blog post titled 'Revival Fire' sat in the drafts folder on the online blog site.

"I didn't know you had a blog."

"It's not mine. It's—" She bit her lip. "It belonged to Emma Dunkirk, the journalist. She died in the explosion last night."

"Crystina, I'm so sorry."

"Ah-huh." She stared at the screen. "Well, someone's going to be sorry, that's for sure."

"So, what exactly are you publishing?"

"Her legacy," Crystina said and clicked 'Publish'.

Seconds later, the hits began to show. Comments expressing their condolences to the one acting on behalf of Emma. Shares across social media platforms: *Finally, some truth in the media,* and, *Here's the real story of what's going on in Juniper City. Praise Jesus!*

Jeremiah shook his head in disbelief. "She has quite the following."

"Had," Crystina corrected. "Since her first article on Azure Blaze, she's been publishing her findings about faith and the history of the church in Juniper. It's fascinating, really."

Jeremiah nestled in closer to see the screen, but Crystina deliberately shifted her chair away.

He swallowed hard. "I know you've had a rough night, but anyone would think you're trying to avoid me."

She stared unblinkingly at the screen and a tear ran down her cheek. "I can't lose anyone else, Jerry."

"You won't." He reached for her hand.

She stood up. "I mean it. I can't keep going through this. It's not fair."

His face twisted. "What are you saying?"

"I never should've said what I said the other night." She shook her head. "It was impulsive and selfish and... and..."

"Not true?" he offered.

She slammed the laptop closed. "I just can't do this, okay? And we obviously can't be friends, you've made that very clear." She picked up the laptop and held it to her chest. "So, why don't you just go and be with Harper. There has to be something there, right? Just... just go..."

And with that, Crystina disappeared upstairs.

When he returned his attention to Abuela, she was silently making two cups of tea.

"I don't understand," Jeremiah said. "I thought—"

"Just give her time," Abuela said gently and placed a mug of hot tea in front of him. "She'll come round."

"And what if she doesn't? What do I do then? Do I just pretend I'm not in love with her?"

Abuela smiled to herself before she took a sip of tea. "Tell me, is that the first time you have said that out loud?"

He swallowed hard. They both knew the answer.

"Maybe that's the problem." She shrugged.

"It's not." He stared long and hard into his cup. "I get it, everyone she gets close to, she loses in some way. Even that Xavier. I really didn't see that coming."

"But this isn't about him," Abuela said. "It never was. You know that. Just like *she* knows, it was never really about Harper Lloyd. And, well, she hasn't lost *everyone*."

Jeremiah flashed his lopsided grin. "You're pretty clued in, Abs. But, I screwed up. That's why she thinks I'd be better off without her."

"Jeremiah Sanderson," Abuela began sternly, "Do not pretend to tell me what my granddaughter *thinks*. You know as well as I do, this isn't about Harper, or that man Xavier, it's not even about you, or that lovely girl Emma she spoke of so fondly."

He nodded slowly. "It's about that night."

"Crystina has not had a dream like that since she was a little girl. She has buried it. And she has never understood why she was the only one to survive," Abuela said, then asked him, "Jeremiah, have you ever been to confession?"

"No ma'am, it's not something we really do in my church."

"Well, I believe confession is good for the soul." She nodded thoughtfully. "You see, I know that God has cleansed me with the blood of Jesus Christ. I know I am forgiven. But sometimes, I need the priest to remind me.

I like to think of it as him holding up a mirror so I can see myself clearly."

"O-kay. And?"

"Jeremiah, right now what Crystina needs from you is for you to hold up a mirror. Part of her knows now why she survived that night, to become Azure Blaze. But she needs you to remind her. This isn't just her calling. If you want to be with her, as I know you do, then it is yours too."

The chair skidded back as Jeremiah stood. "Okay. Mirror."

She nodded once. "Mirror."

Then Jeremiah turned and ran upstairs.

Crystina sat on the floor of the lantern room, photos strewn around her, and the burner phone in pieces beside her. She hadn't asked for this. She just wanted to go on a ride to remember her Papi.

Mama's smile shone bright off the first photo she picked up. She was smelling a sunflower. Dad must have taken it because there was a spark in Mama's eyes as she looked toward the person holding the camera. A light. The light of love glinted in those eyes. Crystina knew that look all too well. It was the way Jeremiah gazed at her; and that terrified her.

She flicked through pictures of Jacob eating spaghetti—as the first child, everything was captured multiple times. There were fewer photos of Anthony and even fewer of Matthew. Then there was Crystina. The bright-eyed girl in a princess dress and patent leather shoes who'd rather get her frilly socks muddy than miss out on the fun. There was a photo of her set in front of Papi on his motorbike and once again she was reminded of the call that had been thrust upon her.

"Why couldn't I just be in heaven with them?" she prayed aloud. "Why couldn't you have taken me too? Someone else could have been Azure Blaze and I wouldn't have to live with this... this... this *guilt!*" She threw the pile of photos across the lantern room and pulled her knees up to her chest, sobbing. "I can't do this, Lord! I can't do this alone! Who am I? Emma believed in someone who doesn't even exist." She sighed. "Anyway, revival in this city seems impossible when there are men like Lee Bernard who literally get away with murder. Why, Lord?" She sobbed into her knees. "Why..."

A hand rested on her shoulder; strong, unmoving, and warm. As she sobbed, she breathed in the scent of soap, fresh laundry, and a hint of Old Spice. Part of her wanted to flinch away, to tell him to leave and never return. But there was something about the heat exuding from him, like a flame igniting her skin and melting parts of her she hadn't realized needed to thaw.

She told herself she'd lose him if she let him get too close. That she knew God was Sovereign, but He had allowed so much tragedy in her life, what was one more loss in His big plan? She told herself that Jeremiah Sanderson didn't belong with her but the seemingly perfect girl he had given himself to just one summer before. She told herself she didn't love Jeremiah Sanderson. But she knew that was a lie.

Still hiding her face in her knees, she felt him kneel beside her.

"Crystina," he began gently, "you were saved for a purpose, you know that, right?"

She nodded.

"Look at me."

She peered up; her face drenched in tears.

"You are Azure Blaze," he said. "And I am so proud of you. And God is too. You're His daughter and He loves you... And I—"

He let out a breathy laugh.

She sniffled. "Yes?"

"And I love you," he said gently. "Always and forever."

"Even though I push you away?"

He flashed his old lopsided smile. "Even then."

"Even though I told you to be with someone else?"

"Eh." He shrugged. "You didn't mean it."

"Even though you'll have to... you know, *wait*."

He bit his lip. "Crystina, look at me."

She met his dark stare.

"I will wait for our wedding day to *kiss* you, if you tell me to," he said, then added, "but it may mean I'll propose to you tomorrow." He chuckled.

Her smile shone like a rainbow through the tears. "Well, that's just crazy."

"Yeah, maybe I should wait a week, huh?"

"No, I mean..." she sniffled, "waiting until our wedding day to kiss me."

Jeremiah's gaze fell to her lips. His jaw pulsed. "Crazy, hey?"

"Yeah. Totally crazy."

"Well, we better rectify that then..."

He gently cupped her bruised jaw with one warm hand and lingered a moment, his eyes drifting closed. Crystina could feel his trembling breath on her cheek. Her eyes fluttered closed as he tentatively brushed her lips with his own. Her head felt light; her body aflame and awakened at once. She took a sharp breath before his mouth gently claimed hers once more. Then he pulled away and rested his forehead against hers.

She released a shaky breath. "I love you," she whispered. "And I want to be with you. Always and forever."

He grinned. "I was hoping you might say that."

CHAPTER 24

Facing Fear

The next time Crystina was summoned to JCPD Headquarters, she was taken to an office she'd never seen before. This one was light, airy. Grayscale family portraits in glass frames lined the desk where Kendra sat shifting salad around in a take-away container.

"Azure Blaze, come in." Striking the last few keys, she clicked once and then settled back in her chair. "Take a seat."

Crystina slowly veered to the chair directly opposite Kendra's, watching her all the while. "Nice office."

"Thanks. This is my personal office. The other one is just for business meetings," Kendra said. "Look, I understand you must have a lot of questions."

"You could say that." She toyed with the felt on the arm of the office chair. "If I hadn't said anything, would you have killed him?"

"Straight into it then." Kendra exhaled loudly and her mouth fell into a pout. "Believe it or not, I don't know."

Crystina waited silently.

"For the first time in my career, I froze," Kendra went on. "All my training evaporated. I meant to *stop* him but... You see, in the moment, in the struggle, some protective, you may even call it maternal, instinct took over." She shook her head. "Azure Blaze, I may look put together in this role, but I can tell you, the honest truth is that I allowed fear to distract me; for the first time in almost fifteen years. Because in that moment, I was absolutely terrified of him hurting you."

"Me?"

"You're Azure Blaze!" Kendra emphasized her point with outstretched hands. "Do you have any idea what that *means*? How it's impacting our city? Do you know what the students at my kids' school are talking about? It's all about how cool it is that we have a hero from God."

Crystina was speechless.

"Do you know how many of those kids are now going to church? Street kids. Kids from the wrong side of everywhere are suddenly coming to church. *My* kids want to drag me to church. And not just that, what do you think you mean to the women of Juniper City? The ones who lived in fear when these attacks started, but don't have to anymore because they know God is watching over them and He's using you to tangibly do that."

Crystina continued to sit motionless as the words washed over her.

"I'm ashamed of myself for not knowing who and what Xavier was. It's my job to know. I knew things weren't adding up at Legion. Not that there was a crumb of evidence left by the time our I.T. department got there. And I'm ashamed of myself that that poor girl died under that bridge because she was so convicted by the Spirit of God that she would not bend to the will of man, and *my* team couldn't save her."

Tears spilled from Crystina's eyes.

"But you." She pointed at Crystina. "You have nothing to be ashamed of, you hear? You did your best out there. You were willing to put yourself on the line to save someone else. Greater love has no man than to lay his life down for his friends, right?"

"Right," she whispered.

"What I'm trying to say is—" Kendra sighed. "You did good, and I am *so* proud of you."

As Crystina stared at her, she imagined her mama saying those exact words about her. She imagined her mama's sweet voice singing for Crystina's little light to shine. She was doing good, her light was shining, and her mama would be so proud of her.

"So as a thank you, from JCPD to you, I have a surprise for you," Kendra said.

Crystina blinked up at her. "Oh, you didn't have to—"

Kendra held up her hand as she stood. "Stop. You really don't want to go saying that. Trust me."

Curious, Crystina followed Kendra down the familiar hallway toward the door that she knew led to the training arena. But Kendra turned instead and continue through to another room, still under passkey, that led to another smaller space. She flicked a switch. Fluorescent lights shuddered awake. There in the blinding white light stood a pitch-black sports bike with sapphire flames down the sides. Beside it, on a single chair, lay armored motorcycle gear.

Crystina's mouth fell open. "I... I don't know what to say."

Kendra strode forward. "The jacket is bullet proof." She grinned then pointed. "Over there's your own roller door that has a ramp that leads down to the underground carpark. And through that door there, there's a small office if you need a quiet place to think or, you know, pray."

She went to the bike and ran her hand over the fresh gloss finish before noticing the registration plate: AZURE-01.

"You're serious?"

"You have a place here with the JCPD if you want it," Kendra said. "It took a little convincing, of course, but once I explained to the board, they were happy to make the most of your *gift*."

Her brow furrowed. "I can't guarantee God will keep speaking to me like that."

"Azure Blaze, if there's one thing I've learned it's that *few* things are guaranteed in this life."

"What about the people who know who I am? I rode without my helmet the other day. Technically, I broke the law."

"Yes, you did, *technically*. But as far as people seeing you, the strangest part was that no one was prepared enough to take a photo. Our IT team found nothing online. Not even security footage. Not to mention the fact that your personnel file at Legion Media International's HR department has mysteriously gone missing, so there is nothing tying you to that place besides hear-say."

"What about Lee Bernard?"

"We'll get him one day. We conducted a full investigation—which was how our team managed to erase your employment history. Juniper City is a big place and you're just one face among millions. It would take a lot for someone to recognize you."

"So..." She glanced around at the shed-like room in disbelief. "I'm employed by the JCPD?"

She folded her arms. "No. Technically, you're an independent specialized unit who is a sort of subcontractor to JCPD."

"Which means?"

"Basically, you're employed by us. Just not on paper."

"So, let me get this straight, I'll get *paid* to hang out here and to go ride a brand-new motorbike?" Crystina said with a hint of a smile.

"Let's just say," Kendra began, "we're giving you the benefit of the doubt that your gift will continue to aid us in our fight against evil in this city."

Crystina nodded. "Well, that sounds like a great job opportunity."

When the sun descended on Juniper Bay and the beacon had been lit. When she could hear Abuela praying by her bedside with Chizzy snoring on the rug. When it was both dark enough and light enough, Crystina left her armored gear and motorbike in the garage and walked across to the Sanderson home. No fear haunted her steps—not the fear of strangers in the dark, nor the ocean crashing beyond. After all, the night was balmy and full of possibility. Like she'd done so many times before, she waded through the wild grass to his window. She knocked and waited.

"Hey." Jeremiah leaned his elbows on the ledge. "I wasn't expecting you."

"What are you doing?"

"Preparing a sermon." He rolled his eyes. "Can you believe it? Want to come in?"

"No, I um..." She glanced away. "I was actually going to see if you wanted to swim but we can do it another time."

"Baby, we can do it *now*." He eased the window all the way up and kicked his legs over the sill. "Only, don't you keep me out too late or the Watchman will have my head."

"The Watchman?"

"Yeah." He landed with a thump and took her hand. "He asked me to preach at St Peter's next Sunday as a guest preacher, but he wants a draft of my sermon as soon as possible so we can work through it together."

She smiled up at him. "That sounds like a great opportunity."

"I hope so."

"So what are you preaching on?"

"Elijah. That's all I know so far."

"What do you mean?"

He shrugged as they walked on. "That's all God's given me so far. So I'm praying and reading and listening."

She squeezed his hand. "I'm proud of you, Jerry."

Pulling her hand to his mouth, he kissed it.

When they reached the water, Jeremiah slipped off his shirt and waded in his shorts. Crystina followed, fully clothed in her jean shorts and her dad's old band t-shirt.

"No bathers?"

She shook her head and grinned. "I have to be careful around you."

He chuckled. "I don't blame you. But you realize you look amazing in anything, right?"

"Well, you should see my new bullet proof jacket from the JCPD."

"*What?*"

"And... my new motorbike." She bopped under the surface, collected water in her mouth, and sprayed him.

He cringed, but it slipped into a crooked grin. "You know that's gross, right?" He then swiped the surface of the water, splashing her. "So, new bike? And yet you *walked* to my place tonight?"

"Yeah." She beamed. "I know I'm Azure Blaze to a lot of people but sometimes I just want to be me. Especially with you."

He reached up to brush strands of wet hair from her face. "Come on, let's go for a swim. Climb on..."

Jeremiah turned and Crystina wrapped her arms around his neck. He gently launched into the water, taking her deeper into the bay. In the distance, the lights of Juniper City glimmered and although the air still clung to the faint taste of ash, the saltiness of the ocean was slowly washing it away. And here in this moment, beneath the moonlight, Crystina finally knew what it was not to be afraid.

"God's got you," she whispered, "you know that, right?"

"Yeah, I do." He turned in the water to admire the view of the cityscape. "He's got *us*."

"I used to be so scared out here. It's so strange to think that all those years ago, if I hadn't been a clumsy six-year-old, I would have..."

"But you *were* a clumsy six-year-old," Jeremiah said softly. "And thank God you were."

"I think I'm ready," she said.

"Are you sure? It's pretty deep here."

She nodded. "Yeah, it's okay."

Then a cool breeze skimmed the water, reminding her that autumn would soon be on its way and that there was a season for everything under heaven. A time to weep and a time to laugh. A time to mourn and a time to dance. And this was her time.

Swim to Me.

Crystina loosened her grip around Jeremiah's shoulders and sprang back into the water. Her heart thumped in her ears so she leaned back and put them under the surface of the water to dull the sound. Her hands swirled through the warm water. Her legs extending and retracting like a dance. She floated and gently swam a little further out until the light of the beacon found her, blinding her with bright white light.

It almost unsteadied her. In her mind she was taken back to that little girl, frozen in the water, fighting to stay in the spot she knew would light up when the beacon came around once more.

But something had changed. *She* had changed. She wasn't frightened anymore.

Crystina gazed at the constellations overhead. "Remember when we took general science because we both needed an extra subject?"

Jeremiah swam closer. "I remember Mr. Munro giving us detention for passing notes."

She smiled at the memory. "But do you remember using the Bunsen burner?"

"Yeah, of course, with the test tubes and stuff."

"It had an 'azure blaze'," she said. "It was blue because it was hotter than a regular flame."

"That's correct, Miss Santos. Ten points for you."

"I want to be like that too." Tears slid down her temples and into the great expanse around her. "I want to live like that. I want to thrive and be like a blue flame."

Jeremiah reached out and threaded his warm fingers between hers. "It's been there all along, hasn't it? Your calling. Just waiting for you."

"And so has yours."

CHAPTER 25

"Cut Them Down"

Nightmares infiltrated Crystina's sleep in the early hours of Sunday morning. Screams echoed through her memory. Haunted by the terror in her mother's eyes, the last thing Mama had seen was her baby girl fall backward into the sea. One clumsy move had saved Crystina's life. God had created her with those two left feet to keep her safe that night. She never thought the constant curse of runs in her opaque white stockings and mud smeared on her prettiest blue dress were in fact blessings.

The power of the flames heated her cheeks. She squinted against it, not wanting to tear her eyes away from the burning wreckage floating on the water. She searched for fellow survivors, for her family to bop to the surface one by one like a favorite lost ball and announce it was a cruel joke.

But there was only one body she could see floating lifelessly.

Jeremiah.

She shook her head and searched for the power she knew lived within her, the power of the Spirit of God.

"You're a liar," she told the darkness. "God's Word calls you the father of all lies. You are a liar!" She screamed as she floated on the fluid abyss. Then a smile broke through the pain. "He wasn't there. He was never there on that boat." She shook her head. "So don't you dare think you can make me doubt my Heavenly Father who has control over *everything*. You have no power here in my mind. Do you hear me?! You have no power here because I am a daughter of God! Jesus Christ died for me and resurrected from the dead. And now the Holy Spirit lives inside of me. So don't you dare think you can mess with me and get away with it."

Her body lifted, hovering over the waters of the deep. And as she viewed the boat from above, she saw the broken mast lying flat, engulfed in fire. But even in the dark, even in the flame, the mast was in the unmistakable shape of a cross.

Crystina lunged forward. Her cheeks burned. Her heart pounded. But not in fear. No, not this time. This time adrenaline coursed through her as the Spirit of God moved.

Wrapping a wool blanket around her pajamas, she descended the stairs by two then burst out of the lighthouse and onto the lawn bare foot. She followed the sandy path toward the water. The moon was full. Its glow accented the waves as they rolled toward her. Salt invaded her senses, much like it had that night in the water. But now there was no fear. Salt was good. She was called to be salt and light to the earth. But first, she had to deal with the enemy who was trying to convince her that salt and light were dangerous, that they had led to fear and death. That she had been called, but there would be consequences. There would be conditions.

"Nice try," she told the darkness. Her toes curled in the cool sand. "But you don't scare me. Not anymore!"

A wind swept over the ocean toward her, tousling her hair and freeing the blanket so it fell to the sand. She stepped forward. The wind kissed her face. She spread her arms out wide and closed her eyes.

"You can't touch me!" she shouted. "See, I'm surrounded! I'm surrounded by the Spirit of God!"

Her skin was on fire. Tingles shot through her in every direction.

"Jesus has the victory over you, devil!" Crystina shouted till her voice gave way, then she said softly, "He has already beaten you. He created the sea and everything in it. There is nothing in this ocean that bows to you. All of creation is waiting for the Kingdom of God. All of creation is groaning. And it doesn't matter what you do, because one day everything is going to be made new. And even if I forget, even if I can't worship because I'm not strong enough." She cleared her throat and found her voice. "Even then, if I can't voice the power of Jesus Christ... then the ocean *will* cry out."

Waves rose and crashed over the rocky cliffs of the lighthouse and Crystina gazed in wonder as the clouds receded to reveal a brilliant constellation of stars above. The beacon's light would veil them for a moment before they came into full view once more.

"You can't compete with the God of the universe." She beamed. "And it is God who is on my side." Then the Holy Spirit returned the words of Psalm 118 to her heart. Her mind had little recollection but her mouth opened and the words poured out. *"The Lord is with me... I will not be afraid. What can mere mortals do to me?"* She dipped her toes into the water. *"The Lord is with me; he is my helper. I look in triumph on my enemies..."* She took a step forward, the cool water swirling about her ankles. *"It is better to take refuge in the LORD than to trust in humans. It is better to take refuge in the LORD than to trust in princes."* Crystina was drawn deeper into the water till she was wading, the waves crashing against her waist. *"All the nations surrounded me, but in the name of the LORD I cut them down."* She smiled as she turned her face toward the moonlight. She remembered the covenant the LORD had made with

Abraham, Isaac, and Jacob. She remembered how He had defended the Israelites and worked miracles on their behalf. She remembered Him bringing them to the promised land and there, when the Israelites were confronted by their enemy, He cut them down. *"They surrounded me on every side, but in the name of the LORD I cut them down..."*

Then she remembered the testimony of Jesus Christ. She remembered the new covenant brought into being through His sacrifice. She and Abuela remembered each morning as they took the bread and the wine, the body and the blood. They remembered that through the resurrection of Jesus Christ they were all part of the people of God; the family of God. Because of the resurrection of Jesus Christ, they had hope, and could look forward to the day when He reunited them with their family.

The water rose to Crystina's neck and she ducked beneath the surface. Opening her eyes, she swam toward the moonlight. Fear niggled at her, but she forced it back. Fear had no place here anymore. Muffled waves were a familiar sound; they had accompanied her all those years ago when her greatest nightmare had become her reality.

She shook her head to dislodge the anxious thoughts, to keep them from making her mind their home. "Not today," she claimed, bursting through the surface of the water. *"I was pushed back and about to fall,* but the LORD helped me. *The LORD is my strength and my defense.*" She looked back at the lights of Juniper City and the light of the beacon guarding the bay. "*He has become my salvation.*"

There she floated, gazing on the landscape that once ignited so much fear and dread in her. She floated in the place that she thought would be her watery grave all that time ago. Twelve years had passed since that night. It was a long time to carry the weight of guilt and fear. But she had done it. A small girl with a wide load on her small shoulders. She had carried it for too long. Now, she had to leave it at the foot of the cross.

Crystina cast her mind back to the dream the enemy had used to try to shake her and the moment Jesus had redeemed it, carrying her into the sky so she could see what He saw. The enemy might have intended it to harm her, but Jesus meant it for her good. For there, she could see the cross aflame. Her family was safe now. And she had a calling over her life. A purpose too great to be ignored; called to fight for the Kingdom of God, and called to fan into flame the revival fire He was stirring in hearts all over Juniper.

"*You are my God,*" she said, "*and I will praise you; you are my God, and I will exalt you...*" Tears slipped from her eyes and into the water. "*I give thanks to you LORD, for You are good... Your love endures forever...*"

When Crystina returned to the lighthouse, her pajamas saturated through and her hair hanging loose in wet clumps, she found Abuela in her robe awake and waiting on the couch. Melchizedek alert by her feet.

"I was wondering where you went without your motorbike," Abuela said with a mild smile.

Crystina sighed and laughed a moment. But her laughter swiftly turned to tears and Abuela opened her arms wide. She went into them and the warmth of them seeped through the wet.

"I had another nightmare," she whispered, "but this time Jesus helped me rise above it and I saw the mast. It was the shape of a cross. Just resting there across the boat. Burning. And I knew all over again the importance of the resurrection. Because now my family is safe. Papi is safe."

Abuela nodded against her. "Yes, my little warrior, he is. And one day we shall see him again. But do not forget the most important part..."

"What's that?"

"One day you will meet Jesus face to face," Abuela whispered in return. "We may now look forward to the day when we are reunited with our family but in my heart I know Who I want to see most of all. And it's not my beautiful son, my lovely daughter in-law, or those three precious boys. It is not even my Rodriguez, my beloved husband... It is Him. Because before them and after them and all the in-betweens, He was with me through it all. And He loves me so completely that He did not even leave me alone in this. He gave me you." Tears rolled down Abuela's cheeks. "And I know I have not been your mama, but you have been a daughter to me in more ways than I could have dreamed."

A sob caught in Crystina's throat, and she buried her face into Abuela's robe. "I love you so much."

Abuela kissed her hair. "And I love you, which is the only reason why I must tell you two things. First, I am so proud of you." She smiled down at her. "And second... you really must have a bath to ward off a chill."

Crystina laughed and sniffed back her tears. "Yes, Abuela."

CHAPTER 26

Called Away

Crystina's heart ached when she heard Emma Dunkirk's name on peoples' lips as they walked into St Peter's that Sunday morning. It had taken only a week for Emma's final blog to reach thousands, many of whom spilled from the cathedral and out onto the street.

Crystina sat beneath their notice in the front pew, her Kevlar tucked safely back at the lighthouse. Abuela sat beside her and then Jeremiah's family. Jeremiah, however, sat beside the Watchman on the platform.

The pianist finished her final notes of the hymn and the Watchman quietly approached the lectern, leaving Jeremiah alone on the sideline for a few moments. Jeremiah's knee began to bounce. The Watchman used his walking aid for support, then opened a heavy braille Bible, and felt his way across it as he read aloud. He then introduced the Sunday School choir who marched out on cue from behind the curtains. After only a single note on the piano, the children broke into song and Crystina's heart shattered all over again.

"This little light of mine," they sang, *"I'm going to let it shine..."*

As the childhood song washed over her, Abuela clutched her hand and Jeremiah met her gaze. Crystina couldn't hold the tears back anymore. Her spiritual nerves felt exposed in every way. Fragile within herself yet strong in the Lord. She glanced around to see if anyone else was so shaken by the innocent performance, at which point she locked eyes with someone she recognized. Second aisle, three rows back sat Kendra. Beside her was a broad clean-shaven man, dark like her, and three teenage boys. Crystina didn't know whether to laugh or cry. Kendra simply shrugged.

When the song was done and it was time for them to rise in congregational worship, Crystina couldn't voice the lyrics. She was so overwhelmed by the multitude of people around her, lifting their voices. By the sight of Jeremiah on that platform. By the memory of Emma Dunkirk and all it now meant for the people of Juniper City.

Holding onto Abuela's hand, she squeezed her eyes closed.

Lord, what is this place You've brought me to? I feel like a foreigner and yet at home. Is St Peter's supposed to be my church home? Is it supposed to be Jeremiah's, too?

You already know the answer...

She smiled to herself.

Thank You, Jesus. Then please tell him too.

Once the Watchman blessed the elements and the congregation partook of them, Jeremiah approached the lectern and opened his weathered Bible with a thud. Crystina watched carefully for his shuddering breath.

Please, Lord. Help him.

Then Jeremiah pushed his shoulders back. "Turn with me to first Kings chapter eighteen..."

Shivers burst down Crystina's arms as she listened to Jeremiah deliver the word from the Lord. It was a passage she'd heard preached hundreds of times—Elijah at Mt Carmel—but somehow hearing it from Jeremiah's mouth as the Holy Spirit directed him, she discovered it in a new way. Her mind and heart were once again blown wide open to the picture of fire barreling down from heaven and igniting a sacrifice with all the odds stacked against it. Three times the altar and the wood had been drenched so the water ran down and into the surrounding trench. According to man and every logical thought, the fire should not have lit. Not to mention the fact that the fire came from no man's effort.

Then she realized, the Lord was revealing a picture of herself. She was the sacrifice. She had almost drowned. As a mere child she had defied all odds of survival, seemingly lost in that partly frozen bay for hours on end. The doctors couldn't explain it. Now, however, Crystina could see the supernatural links, she could see that her miracle was a direct result of her prayer warrior of an Abuela who had always battled on her knees for her.

As Jeremiah's sermon ended, Crystina felt a familiar stirring she'd come to know. A faint breeze drifted from a nearby stained window with its levered glass slightly ajar. Sunlight danced through the colorful pane, bringing to life the picture of Jesus calming the sea.

Then a voice so inaudible and yet so clear told her. **Go. Now.**

Surely not in the middle of a church service?

But the voice was insistent.

So she whispered a swift, "I gotta go," to Abuela and weaved her way back through the crowd of congregants.

Then, she ran.

There was no time to double back and get her bike. An intense urgency spurred her onward and she knew that she didn't have the strength to run all that way on her own. No, He would have to take over. Her sundress was light. Her sandals slapped the sidewalk as she made it through the outskirts of old Juniper town, the part that hadn't burned to the ground, and she arrived at the edges of Juniper City with its high-rise apartments and townhouses.

Whenever she began to overthink and be too much in her head, she reminded herself of Elijah. She almost felt like Peter who stepped out to meet Jesus on the water. For the briefest moment, he had become so lost in his own head that fear and doubt took over. But nevertheless, he had stepped out onto the water. And so would she. Crystina would remember how the Lord gave supernatural strength to Elijah to outrun that chariot. She would remember how He had given her supernatural strength to outrun that stolen car. She would remember every moment that had led her to this one.

She could see it so clearly and she knew exactly where she needed to be. When arriving at the front doors of Legion International Media, she found them open and ran straight for the stairwell. She lost count of the floors. It didn't matter. Steps, balance, and speed.

Jesus, help me. Help me to know what to do.

Steps. Balance. Speed.

When she finally emerged onto the rooftop, sweating and breathless, there was a woman near the edge of the roof.

"Stop!" Crystina shouted with the last breath she had left in her. Panting, she sprinted toward the woman.

A head of white blonde hair whipped around and Harper's bloodshot eyes met hers. "What are *you* doing here?"

Crystina reached for her. "Please don't do this."

"Oh." Harper looked around. "I'm not... I mean, it's not what you think." She stepped down from the ledge. "Sorry, I just, I come here to think."

Crystina's hand dropped. "Are you sure? God told me to come here."

"Like He cares about me." Harper laughed darkly. "Don't worry though, I won't tell anyone your superhero identity."

"Did you hear what I said?" Crystina asked in all seriousness. "God called me out of church, had me run from old Juniper town and up the stairwell, to tell you—"

Harper glanced around as tears spilled down her cheeks. She pursed her lips. "*What?* What does *God almighty* want to tell me?"

I love her. Even after what she did. I still love her. She is my daughter.

Crystina gasped then swallowed hard. "He loves you. Even after what you did. He still loves you..."

Harper rolled her eyes.

"And you're his daughter."

Then she broke. Harper's face twisted. She bent over clutching her stomach.

Crystina knelt and wrapped her arms around her. "It's okay. Whatever it is, it's going to be okay."

"No, it isn't. It'll never be okay!" Harper sobbed. "You don't get it. You'll never get it."

Crystina held her tighter and whispered, "Try me."

"I can't... I can't... you'll tell him."

"Who? God? He already knows."

"No... Jerry."

Crystina swallowed hard.

She sobbed. "You'll tell him..."

"Either way," Crystina said, "you have to tell someone what's going on. It's clearly eating you alive."

Harper drew back and stared up at her, intensity brewing like storm clouds. "I come up here to think... to think about my baby."

Crystina's breath caught in her chest. "Your—"

"I was pregnant," she said then added, "But don't worry, it's gone now."

Thoughts threatened to overwhelm Crystina and send her into an anxious mess, but she shook her head and remembered that just as Jesus had called Peter out to the waves, He had called her here.

"Harper," she whispered. "I am so sorry for your loss."

Harper fell into Crystina's arms again, clutching them, sobbing into her. "I know this sounds totally bizarre but... being up here, it makes me feel closer to heaven, where my baby is..."

"Why don't you come back to the lighthouse with me?" Crystina asked. "Abuela has been planning Sunday lunch all week."

She sniffled. "Will Jeremiah be there?"

Crystina nodded slowly.

"I can't see him. Not yet. I wanted to tell him about the baby, but then I lost it and, well, that was that."

"How far along were you?" Crystina asked. Part of her didn't want to know but the other part of her knew Harper wanted to share.

"Almost twelve weeks. I keep telling myself the miscarriage was punishment for seducing Jerry."

Crystina took a steadying breath. "That's not the way God works. There are consequences, yes, but... I sense that He is grieving with you."

Harper's sobbing quietened and she whispered, "Really?"

"Yes, of course. He's a good God, Harper. The very fact that He sent me here to you right now is a testament to that truth. He wants you to know that He loves you. So much."

Harper's lip curled.

"Now," Crystina said, "are you going to come and help me eat Abuela's feast or not?"

"I'm not really dressed for it." She shrugged.

"You look amazing in *anything*. It's actually a little annoying." Crystina let out a breathy laugh.

"Thanks, but... Crys, I can't face him. Not now."

"Yes, you can," Crystina said. "You can because he deserves to know that one day when this life is done, and he gets to be with Jesus that there will be a child waiting up there for him. His first child."

The words cut Crystina to the core, but they appeared to be exactly what Harper needed.

She started to nod as she cried, "Okay, let's do this."

The heavy wooden table in the lighthouse's kitchen was almost full again. The Watchman prayed over the Sunday feast from Papi's old seat and even Harper closed her eyes.

"Do you want to tell me what she's doing here?" Jeremiah asked in undertones from the chair beside her.

"She'll tell you soon." Crystina gave his hand a squeeze, treasuring this moment *before*. Before he found out he would have been a father, had the baby made it to full term. Crystina briefly wondered if this would change things between them, but she knew she couldn't dwell on that right now. "By the way, I really enjoyed your sermon this morning."

"Even though you've heard it preached countless times before?"

"You gave it new meaning."

"Well," he said, "I must admit, it did remind me a little of Azure Blaze."

"Oh, really…"

That was when Harper cleared her throat and asked to speak to Jerry in private. Part of Crystina died inside, knowing they had yet another emotional tie.

Jeremiah instinctively looked to Crystina. His brow raised. "Is it okay with you?"

Flutters stirred. "Uh, yeah, of course."

He tugged her hand up and kissed it. "Sure?" he asked again, this time softer. Then his dark eyes locked onto hers. "You're my girl, remember?"

And just like that, every fear melted.

"Yeah, of course," she said. "Go, and good luck, okay. I'll be praying."

He nodded once then followed Harper out the front door.

As Abuela passed her, clearing dishes, she pressed a kiss onto Crystina's hair. "I am proud of you. That would not have been easy."

"I am curious, was she the reason you were called out of the service today?" the Watchman asked.

"Yes," Crystina said. "Yes, it was. I'm sorry. I was so enjoying it."

"There is no need to apologize. As we all know, His ways are greater than our own. Though I am sorry to now be called away myself."

"Oh? Do you have other plans?"

"Yes, indeed." The Watchman leaned heavily on his walking aid as he stood. "Could you do me a favor, Crystina?"

Her chair skidded back. "Of course. Anything."

"It is no wonder He chose you," he muttered, smiling as he hobbled toward the door. "Please read Hebrews thirteen verse two when you have a moment. I would be interested to hear your thoughts."

Crystina nodded slowly.

Abuela reached for her Bible by the front table.

The Watchman turned and looked at Abuela and then straight into Crystina's gaze. "Goodbye. I do hope we meet again."

Then he disappeared out the door.

Crystina and Abuela shared a wide-eyed glance before Abuela began to flick through the pages then settled in the book of Hebrews with a heavy hand.

Crystina leaned over her shoulder. "What does it say?"

Tears sprang to Abuela's eyes.

Crystina searched the black and white printed page to find the following verse: *"Do not forget to show hospitality to strangers, for by so doing some people have shown hospitality to angels without knowing it."*

She gasped and ran to the door. Yanking it open, she sprinted across the lawn to the gravel carpark where Harper and Jeremiah stood, both tear-filled.

"I'm sorry, I... uh..." She shook her head. "The Watchman. Which way did he go?"

"Haven't seen him." Jeremiah sniffled. "He must still be inside."

Crystina's insides shuddered as the realization dawned on her. Then, in the next moment, she paused and looked again at Jeremiah.

She sucked in a breath. "I'm so sorry, Jerry."

He drew to her like a magnet and his large body sank around her. "Praise God you came out when you did. I don't think I can talk about this anymore."

Crystina peered over his shoulder to see a heartbroken Harper kick some gravel before heading back inside. Once alone, she pressed a kiss to Jeremiah's neck and held him tighter.

"Wanna go for a ride?" she asked. "Whenever I feel overwhelmed, it feels good to go for a ride and clear my head."

"Yes," he breathed, and managed a slight smile. "Let's ride."

Book 2 - Preview

By the time autumn swept over Juniper, the Watchman was commanded once again concerning Azure Blaze.

Holy Spirit stirred as an indigo mist around the Daughter of the Most High, beckoning for her attention. But her tear-filled eyes remained steely on the road before her. Her hands gripped the handlebars as though her life depended on it. Perhaps it did? The Watchman was not privy to such things.

But even he could tell her fire was dim, waning beneath the chill of spiritual attack. Demonic spirits chased her motorbike as she powered over the slick mountain roads. The Watchman unsheathed his sword. In the spiritual realm, he could see clearly. Walk with purpose. He was not limited to the human guise he took on in their world. No, he was a warrior of the Most High God and he would defend this daughter should the Almighty give the instruction.

But the commands of the LORD that echoed on the wind did not require a weapon. Not yet at least.

Rather, obediently, the Watchman placed an advisory sign where there was not one before. "Slippery when wet."

But Azure Blaze did not slow down.

The Watchman placed a log in her path.

But Azure Blaze swerved to the wrong side of the road to dodge it. A pair of headlights streamed toward her. A horn blared through the cold night air. He reached for her, and she weaved back beneath his invisible guiding hand.

Rain pelted the pavement and the raging demons stayed on Azure Blaze's wheel, chanting her worst fears over her.

"Jeremiah never loved you. He wants her. He has always wanted her. Today just proves it..."

"No one loves you. You should have died with your family."

"Amos Xavier was right about you."

And perhaps the worst of all: *"Emma's death was your fault..."*

In one last attempt, the Watchman stepped out of the shadows, his sword now a walking aid beside him, his vision dimming into that of the blind preacher as he lingered at the edge of the pine forest, soaked from the downpour.

He felt Azure Blaze's stare. She would know what and who he truly was. Surely, she would see him and pull over. Surely, he could speak life over her and then send these spirits of darkness back where they belonged.

But all his presence did was steal her concentration.

Sensing her vulnerability, one demon kicked her back tire, and it slid out. Another seized the opportunity and threw her from the motorbike. Then, another, invigorated by her scream, tossed her body along the ground, and relished in the sound of her bones snapping.

The Watchman wanted to go to her. But he waited on the command of the LORD. Waited. And waited.

But no command was given.

Then, another demon hovered over Azure Blaze—the Daughter of God—and thrust his fists into her until her head rolled back unconscious.

ENOUGH.

The tormentors shrieked and scampered away.

I AM had spoken.

With Azure Blaze barely alive, the Watchman returned to his angelic form, sheathed his sword, and knelt beside her mangled body. Then, he listened for the command of YAHWEH.

The voice that followed was not the divine avalanche that crushed the demonic spirits and sent

253

them scattering in fear. No, this voice was as gentle as the cool breeze skimming the waterfall of the rock face, as delicate as the pine needles shifting and spreading their sweet scent.

Bring my daughter to Me.

FIND OUT WHAT HAPPENS TO AZURE BLAZE IN BOOK TWO.

Acknowledgements

Jesus, thank You for taking me on this adventure! I cannot wait to see what You have planned for this book series. I'm so grateful to write a character like Azure Blaze.

Thank you to my beta readers – Jenny, Clarity, Rob, and Tiffany. I am so grateful for your encouragement and feedback.

Thank you to the beautiful community that is the Christian Mommy Writers who have helped me in countless ways, and who notably brainstormed with me to come up with the name "Azure Blaze".

Thank you to Sarah Everest for polishing this book for me, your advice has been invaluable.

To Wendy, thank you for praying for me and for reminding me that writing is indeed a ministry. And an important one at that.

Lastly, thank you to Daniel for being my sounding board. And to H for napping, so your mama could actually have the time to write this book.

www.ingramcontent.com/pod-product-compliance
Lightning Source LLC
Chambersburg PA
CBHW070000120726
47909CB00003B/764